TO RAZOR RU
BABY RUCKUS
HOPE YOU ENJOY THIS BOOK.

Amanda Moonstone

The Missing Prince

Dan Wright

Illustrations by Kirsten Moody

DAN WRIGHT
(THE VIP OF MC'S!)

Originally published February 2015 by Paper Crane Books.

Second printing. Published by Pandragon Publishing

To contact the author please email
pandragonpublishing@gmail.com

ISBN: 978-1514345481

By the Same Author

<u>Draconica Series</u>

Trapped on Draconica
The Wandering Valkyr
All Hail Emperor Gothon
Taurok's War
Legacy of the Dragonkin
Final Ragnarok: She Returns

<u>Comics</u>

Countdown to Final Ragnarok
Draconica: Zarracka Dragonkin

<u>Other</u>

Death on Valentine's Day, a short story featured in Recollection of
Shared Days

Dedicated to my friends and family. Thanks for believing in me :)

And to all the Monkeybadgers out there.

Draconica is the world in which the stories of *Amanda Moonstone* take place. It is so named after the creatures that made it—the dragons. Powerful creatures with immense knowledge and mystique. Now they are extinct, but their legends remain.

When Draconica was first created and life was breathed into the world, the dragons discovered a source of great power at the core of the planet. Kerrigal, the most knowledgeable of all the dragons, named this power magic, and he taught it to the mortals of Draconica to use in their everyday lives. This was known as The Age of Sorcery.

However, magic by its very nature was unpredictable and not very easy to control—and as such it raged out of control. The dragons, not wanting their world destroyed, taught the mortals to use the natural resources of their planet to create things. And so, The Age of Science began as the mortals learned technology and masonry—allowing them to build cities, medicines, armour and weapons. Overtime, their reliance on magic disappeared.

These days, magic is all but forgotten and many mortals distrust it. Those that do practice it are often looked down upon in society. Though not practiced, its influence still exists. But true magic cannot be harnessed by mortals directly, due to its corrupting influence, therefore they must learn to use it through the use of magical items such as dragon gems. Only certain mortals have the latent ability to control such items.

Amanda Moonstone is one of them.

This adventure is set in the Kingdom of Celtland, the neighboring land to Brittana. Previously ruled by the benevolent Queen Sheena Gryphenpyre, the land is now commanded under the iron fist of King Kimera Gryphenpyre. For six years he has ruled the country through fear and loathing—and no one has been able to challenge his reign.

Until now . . .

Prologue

A Prince in Hiding

Watergate Pass Village

"**D**aryl, dinner's ready!"

Daryl put down his book and headed to the dining room where Glenda, his mother, was serving dinner. The smell of beef stew filled the air. Glenda had already set three places at the table: one for Daryl, one for her, and one for her husband of twenty years. He worked as a woodcutter and often spent most of his time in the forest. Glenda never complained though—she enjoyed this life as long as it meant spending time with Daryl.

"Smells nice, Mother," Daryl said, taking his place at the table, and brushing back his blond hair.

Glenda ladled stew from the pot into Daryl's bowl. "Eat up," she said.

1

"Shouldn't we wait for Father?" Daryl asked.

"He'll be working late tonight and has asked us to start without him." She filled her bowl with stew and then set the pot on the fire to keep it warm before taking her place at the table.

Daryl took a sip of the stew and winced as it burned his tongue.

"Careful."

He waited a few seconds for his tongue to cool down and then slurped his food again. It was a simple meal; he knew his mother wished she could provide better for him, but Daryl never complained.

"Hey, Mum?"

"Yes, sweetheart?"

"I was just reading about Queen Sheena."

Glenda's heart jumped a beat upon hearing the name, and she had to smile to hide her nervousness. "Really?"

"Yeah. From what I read, she sounded like a really nice lady. The book said she always gave money to the poor and even offered food to them when they needed it. She must have been a great ruler."

Glenda sighed. "Those were happier times."

"How did she—*you know*?"

"They say she was set upon by bandits. She had no chance."

"I wish I'd met her."

Glenda hoped that Daryl wouldn't ask too many questions about the Queen. Some secrets should remain hidden.

The door to their house burst open. Glenda spun round, only to find her husband framed in the doorway. "Marcus, you scared me!"

Marcus was a burly man with a thick moustache and a strong, chiseled jaw. His eyebrows were pushed up to the top of his forehead and the veins on his neck pulsated as he as he struggled to catch his breath.

"Marcus, what's wrong?"

"K . . . K . . ." Marcus struggled to breathe, having run from the woods. The woods were not far from the village—but what Marcus had seen coming towards them forced him to move with all speed whilst he still had time. "Kimeran soldiers!"

Glenda stood, turning white as a sheet, and knocked over her dinner plate in the process. "*Here?*"

They'd feared this day would come. "They can't find him here! I'll keep them distracted."

"Marcus . . ."

"Glenda, please! Get Daryl to safety." Without another word, Marcus charged out of the house.

Glenda's heart leapt in her chest, her eyes blurred with tears. She turned to her son, saying words she'd prayed she'd never have to: "Pack your things, quickly."

"Mum? What's going on?"

"Please, there's no time to explain."

Glenda helped Daryl pack a few supplies of food and water into a small pack, shoving them in without any care if the items fit or not. Then she pulled aside the dinner table and lifted up the rug that was underneath it. Though it did not reveal anything untoward at first, Glenda grabbed the sides of two floorboards and lifted them up, revealing a fairly small and dank smelling hole. "Quickly, Daryl, get in there."

"What is it?"

"It's a tunnel that will take you out of the village," Glenda replied. She and Marcus had dug this tunnel themselves in secret—for this very eventuality. "Come, there isn't much time."

Daryl had to be practically pushed into the opening, despite some protesting. Once he was in, Glenda lifted up the floorboards.

"Wait!" Daryl shouted.

"Follow the path," Glenda told him. "It will take you outside the village. Get as far away from here as you can."

"What about you and Dad? Aren't you coming?"

"We'll be right behind you," Glenda said. "Please just go." She planted a kiss on his forehead, tears in her eyes. "I love you so much . . . just run, run while you can."

"Mum?"

Glenda slammed down the floorboards, making sure they were securely in place and replaced the rug. Wiping her eyes clean, she tidied the house, making sure nothing looked out of place. She hoped Daryl could get away in time.

They rode into the village on dark horses, the moonlight glinting off their silver armour. Each wore a green surcoat bearing the symbol of the Gryphenpyre Household, the ruling monarchy of Celtland. The villagers huddled in fear and confusion as the soldiers flooded in, cutting off any escape routes.

Glenda joined her husband, giving him a subtle nod to confirm Daryl was safe. Marcus smiled.

A Prince in Hiding

One solider dismounted. He was a large, muscular man that had seen more war than most people had eaten hot dinners. A scar marred his face and disappeared behind a thick brown beard. He stepped towards the crowd. "Who is in charge here?"

The people of the village huddled together, each afraid to come forward. Marcus sucked in a deep breath, steeled himself, and stepped forward despite his wife's attempts to hold him back. "I am."

The soldier eyed him up and down. Marcus stood resolute, determined to show no fear, though inside he was trembling. When the soldier seemed satisfied, he turned to address a mounted figure. "This one said he is in charge, Your Majesty."

"Thank you, Captain Luthar," spoke a snide voice.

Atop a black horse, who seemed barely able to support the rider's girth, sat King Kimera Gryphenpyre. He was dressed in green and silver robes that barely concealed his podgy belly, and his thick green cape hung heavily against the horses flank. His hair was short and dark and he bore a small moustache and a weak beard. His eyes carried an air of pomposity and egotistical flair that few could match.

From his horse, he looked down towards Marcus with a sneer. "It is customary to bow before your King," he glowered.

Marcus swallowed hard, but bowed none the less. Kimera's cruelty was legendary. He would have anyone executed just for looking at him in the wrong way. He was *nothing* like his sister.

"Your Majesty," Marcus said, trying to feign ignorance as to why the King was here. "Welcome to our village."

"Do you hear that, Luthar?" Kimera asked the Captain. "He welcomes us to his village. How polite. And we are honoured to be here in this . . . *hovel* of yours. We're after some information—and I think you may be able to tell us what we need to know."

He clicked his fingers at Luthar, who pulled out a piece of paper and shoved it at Marcus. On it was a picture that looked like a bear with wings. "Six years ago, a baby was brought to this village bearing this birthmark on his leg."

Marcus studied the picture and tried to hide his reaction as he lied through his teeth. "There . . . are no children that have that mark here."

"Really?" Kimera leaned closer and glared at Marcus from atop his horse, almost tumbling over. "Are you . . . quite . . . sure?"

"I am, Your Majesty."

Prologue

Kimera stroked his moustache, a wicked grin curling the corners of his lips. "See, here's the thing. I know that you are lying. So, I will ask you one more time—*Where is the child?*"

Marcus tried to hold his nerve. Behind him, his wife could barely keep still, her hysterics somewhat obvious to anyone that cared to look in her general direction.

"Have it your way," Kimera snarled. "Search the village!"

The soldiers tore through the village, searching every nook and cranny of every house, seeing if they could find either the child or some hiding place for him. They pushed over furniture, pushed over cupboards and tore up carpets without any care for the villagers' property. The villagers huddled in the town square, guarded whilst the soldiers searched—many of which complained when they saw their house being destroyed. Their protests were usually responded to by a fist or a blow from the butt of one of their swords. The first time Luthar saw this, he tried to step in to stop it—but Kimera held up a hand to stop him. "Let them do their job."

Luthar cursed silently inside his mind. They were supposed to be his guards, but he seemed to have little to no power over them anymore. Not since Kimera started to throw his weight around.

Glenda and Marcus's house was the last one for the guards to go in. From outside, they could hear their furniture being smashed and possessions being thrown to the ground as if they were worthless. Both of them hoped they would not find the secret tunnel. They had gone to great pains to make sure the floorboards looked exactly like the rest so as to not stand out.

Eventually, the noise from within stopped. Marcus and Glenda held hands and kept their breath still as the guards exited their home.

"Well?" Kimera asked.

"Nothing, Sire," one of the guards replied.

Both Glenda and Marcus let out a subtle sigh of relief. They hadn't found the tunnel.

"*What?*"

"We searched everywhere, but we could not find him."

"Where is he?" Kimera growled at Marcus. "Where have you hidden him?"

"We don't know what you're talking about," Marcus shouted, finding some hidden bravery. "Leave us alone, you sick—"

His defiance was ended by a blow from the hilt of a soldier's sword to his chest. He went down on his knees. "MARCUS!" Glenda rushed to her husband's side.

"You are either very brave—or very stupid to speak to me that way, *peasant*!" Kimera spat. "Tell me where the child is!"

"Please!" Glenda pleaded. "We don't know about any child. I swear. Please, we haven't done anything wrong."

Kimera looked down at Glenda as she tearfully pleaded for the safety of the village. A deathly silence filled the air as everyone waited for his response.

"Fair enough," Kimera replied. "Captain, we didn't find what we were looking for. Let's move on."

The King turned his horse around, seeming to leave. The village breathed a collective sigh of relief.

"Oh, and Captain . . ." Kimera turned back to Luthar. "Have the village razed."

"Sire?" Luthar gasped.

"Did I stutter? I gave you an order."

"B-but Sire . . . ," Luthar protested. "These villagers are no threat."

"They held a fugitive for six years," Kimera sneered. "We must teach them a lesson—and make an example of those who defy the crown."

"But . . . Your Majesty."

"Luthar . . . are you disobeying an order from your *King*? You know that would be classed as treason. And you know what will happen if you don't do what I say."

Luthar bit his tongue and clenched his fist. He hated having to give this order—but he was the Captain of the Royal Guard and the King's word was law. He had no choice but to obey.

Sheena, forgive me.

"Burn the village!" he shouted. "Burn everything!"

Daryl watched from afar, hidden behind a clump of trees that looked out on his village. He watched as the hungry flames grabbed at the wooden huts, and heard the screams of his people inside. He watched as it turned to ash, the wind gusting the flames in his direction so that he could feel the heat upon his skin.

Prologue

He stayed hidden, hoping his parents would come out. He waited for them—his mother had promised him, after all. She had promised that she and his father would be right behind him.

But they never came, even after the soldiers had left.

The King and his guards watched as the flames took hold of the village, long beyond rescue. They stayed behind in case there were survivors.

There weren't.

"Search every village, town, and city," Kimera growled between clenched teeth. "I want him found."

Luthar gave a quick nod. He felt cold and dirty. He'd never before been asked to do something quite so horrific. Kimera's obsession with the boy was unnatural. This was not what Luthar had planned when he joined the Royal Guard, and now it seemed the whole of the country would feel Kimera's wrath.

An idea struck. "Your Majesty, if I may make a suggestion? Razing villages will only garner the hatred of your people."

"Why should I care about them?" Kimera growled. "They defy me, they should be taught a lesson."

"Yes, but maybe there is an alternative."

"Oh, very well, let's hear it then."

"Put out a missive for the child. Ask the people to help find him—say that he's a lost relative and offer a reward. Gold speaks louder than violence to these people."

"A bounty?" Kimera considered it. "Yes . . . yes that could work. Very well, Captain."

Luthar sighed with relief. Perhaps this way, no more innocents would suffer.

"I'll play on the sensitivity of the common people. After all, who doesn't want to help where a lost child is concerned? Sooner or later, someone will bring him to me."

Chapter 1

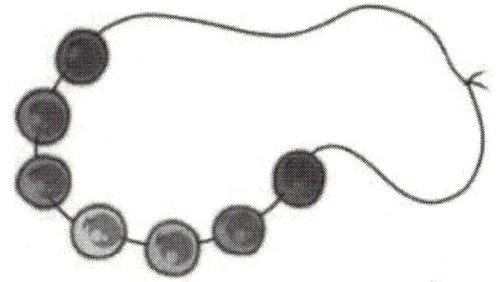

The Struggling Sorceress

Ashfeld

Amanda crushed up ingredients in her bowl, grinding and then mixing them into a thick paste. The mixture was one part each of roseflower and cromiweed, two parts bone dust, and a dash of salt. When she was done, she double-checked the recipe.

"Okay," Amanda mumbled to herself, "now we have to mix it with fresh water and then stir it with some red draught potion—boiled."

She checked the red draught—it had already begun to bubble. She pointed a finger at the glass bottle and the flames increased ever so slightly in response. When she was sure the flame didn't require her attention, she mixed the paste with a vial of water and stirred it until it was thick and syrupy, creating a honey colour. She then pointed

9

towards the red mixture. The glass container hovered in the air, lifted by Amanda's will alone.

She checked the scroll again. "*Add two litres worth of boiling red draught to the mix. Measurements must be exact to get the desired effect.*

"Well, here goes nothing."

The red draught hovered over the vial of syrup. She could barely contain her excitement. If she got the mixture right, this would be a bestseller. She had been desperate to get a hold of the ingredients, and they had not come cheap. It would all be worth it when the potion was complete.

This is the one, she thought. *This is the one that's going to solve all my problems.*

The end of the bottle tipped towards the awaiting syrup, a line of red liquid gradually trickling its way to the end of the bottle.

What would happen? Would there be an explosion—a burst of light? Mixing different potions often had different effects. She held her breath.

A thump at her front door broke her concentration. The red mixture dropped from the air and crashed to the floor, spilling its contents everywhere. Amanda could only stare as her months of preparation had come to naught.

"Rats!"

The thumping on her door continued. Grumbling, Amanda stormed over to see who dared disturbed her work. She put on her best pout and flung the door open.

"Yes?"

When she saw who it was, she instantly regretted her tone.

"Oh . . . er . . . hello, Miss Berger."

Miss Berger was a rotund woman with hair the colour of mouldy parchment. Her face seemed to be permanently etched with disagreement, as if it were impossible for her to smile. She glared at Amanda with fists on her wide hips.

"Er, lovely day we're having," Amanda said, trying to make polite conversation.

"You know what day it is, Moonstone?" Berger crowed.

"Er . . . the last day of the month?"

"It's the first of the month." Berger held out a hand. "Pay up."

Rent. Oh, bother.

"Ah," Amanda stuttered. "Yes . . . you see, there has been a little bit of a drought in sales recently and . . . well, you know, making potions is expensive." She laughed nervously, but Berger's frowning eyebrows and curled lip gave Amanda the impression that she didn't see the humour in that statement. "I need ingredients and . . . well, they aren't cheap."

"You don't have it, do you?"

"Give me just one more month and I *swear* I'll have it."

"That's what you said *last* month, *and* the month before that—and the month before that! In fact, you've said little else for the last *five* months! My patience is wearing thin with you, Moonstone."

"I know—I know . . . I'm sorry, but I promise you, I'm working on a new potion and it's going to be a bestseller!"

Berger gazed into her house towards the potion table. She spotted the broken glass on the floor, and then glanced back to Amanda.

"Er . . . production problems."

"What have I told you?" Berger snapped. "You'll ruin the woodwork! That," she stabbed a pudgy finger towards the mess, "is going on your bill!"

"Really? Oh, come on . . ."

"I've been very kind to you—kinder than I should have been after what you did. I know you had problems, but my patience is wearing thin. One month without paying rent is bad enough, two is unacceptable—but five? Accommodation here isn't free. You either pay rent or you're out."

Amanda was trapped. She tilted her head and narrowed her eyes. "You know . . . you shouldn't mess with a sorceress. Not when she

could use her magic to . . . burn you alive."

Berger glared back, folding her arms, which was a bit of an effort given the layers of fat padding her midsection.

"That was a bad joke," Amanda apologised sheepishly. "But please . . . can't you just give me a little extension? I have some really good stock to sell this time, I promise! Just a little extension is all I ask for."

Berger's glare did not disappear. Amanda had used the same plea before. This time, Berger didn't seem convinced. "You have until the end of the week," she allowed.

"Well, you see, I was kind of hoping for another couple of months or so . . ."

"*End of the week*—production problems or not," Berger stated sternly. "No rent, no home. Take it or leave it."

Berger walked away, a slight waddle in her step.

"Right," Amanda said after her. "End of the week. No problem." She closed the door lightly, sighing.

Amanda checked herself in the mirror before she went to work, her green eyes glinting back at her. She brushed her long chestnut hair over her shoulders, although when she saw the heavy streaks of grey she sighed lamentably. She remembered when it used to be a perfect colour. She wore a purple hood over her dark green dress and around her neck was a gemmed necklace. However, these were no ordinary gems—they were *dragon gems*. Dragon gems were a rare commodity on Draconica and each one contained a magical power that Amanda was able to manipulate. Whilst it did make for a pretty necklace, a lot of people were put off by the magic element— especially given the things that she could do with them.

Happy she was presentable, Amanda took a deep breath and recited her mantra. "I can do this! I can sell to these people! I can make money out of this!" No matter how many times she said it, she never really believed it, but time was of the essence, and she needed to work harder than ever before.

The market of Ashfeld was bustling with hundreds of busy shoppers. This was a good sign for Amanda. With the amount of people that were here today, she could make back the money for rent . . . if she sold to every person here. Easier said than done!

The Struggling Sorceress

She rolled her large cart, filled with any number of potions, to her usual place in the market. She secured her cart and then attached the sign to the side of it which read AMANDA MOONSTONE'S POTIONS: ANY POTION. ANY NEED. She checked her stock, made sure everything was in place, and then took a deep, calming breath. She then flung herself towards the people in the market.

"Step right up, folks! Amanda Moonstone's Potions: Any potion. Any need. If I don't have it, I guarantee I can make one for you. Have a special lady in your life? I've got just the thing for you. Have a complaint? I have the cure! Ladies, worried that the wrinkles in your skin are stopping you from getting that man? My potions will guarantee to keep your complexion as smooth as the day you were born. Step right up folks, come and get them!"

No one paid her any attention.

Amanda had always been a little bit of an outcast in Celtland—on account that she practiced sorcery. Magic had all but been forgotten since The Age of Sorcery came to an end some 4,000 years ago. Those that clung to the old ways were often looked down upon. However, the people were especially suspicious of Amanda after *the incident* a year ago. It was something Amanda was not proud of, but not something people weren't likely to forget. As such, she was lucky to get a look-in, and most walked straight past her stall.

"You, sir! Why not come and take a look? No? How about you, young man? You look like you could use a pick me up! Why not give this a try—it's good for what ails you. Yes, ma'am, why not try some of my special love potion? It will get you any man you want, *promise*. You want to try? No? Okay. I'll be here when you get back . . . I'll be here all day . . . Probably."

It came to the end of the day, and the market had started to die down. Amanda sat behind her cart, taking a quick count of her earnings for the day. She had sold, in total, two potions. The profits would barely cover her for five days rent—let alone five months. It might buy her a loaf of bread, but that was about it.

Well, I've had worse days, I guess.

Amanda knew that staying any longer would be self-imposed torture. She decided to pack up shop and leave, taking what little earnings she had.

"HEY!"

Chapter 1

A giant of a man, with arms as thick as great oak trees, stomped over to Amanda's shop. He looked angry.

"Er, hey . . . how can I help?"

"That love potion you sold me didn't work!" he roared. "You told me that it would make any woman love me!"

"Oh, really?" Amanda tried to sound surprised, but she was never good at lying. Unfortunately, her usual ingredients she used for making love potions had all dried up—and she hadn't been able to get any more—so she had substituted some. Unfortunately, the one ingredient that was essential for this one to work, Amanda could no longer afford. Without it, the potion was useless.

"I want my money back!"

"Ah, well see . . . here is the problem . . . ," Amanda said. "It clearly says on the sign NO REFUNDS."

The man checked the sign. "No it doesn't."

"Yeah, I've been meaning to put that on there."

"I'm not going anywhere until I get my refund!"

The man was making quite a scene and others were starting to notice. Amanda bit her bottom lip, her eyes darted from side to side, hoping that the answer would reveal itself soon. "Listen," she whispered. "I'm . . . kind of in a bit of a bind at the moment . . . so I can't give you a refund right now." She held up a bottle. "Why don't I give you this one for half price instead?"

The man knocked the bottle out of her hand and grabbed her by the sides of her gown. "I'm not going until I get my refund! If you don't have it, I'll just have to take payment some other way . . ."

"Say . . . er . . . You wouldn't hurt a lady would you?"

The monster of a man growled, the stench of his breath making her toes curl.

"I see . . ." Amanda looked around for some way to talk her way out of this. This man looked big enough to crush her with just his little finger.

"The women *laughed* at me!" the man growled. "You promised me that this potion would make any woman fall in love with me. Now I'm going to—" He raised his fist, but stopped at the sound of a *meow* next to him. He glanced down and saw a stray cat wandering near his feet.

The man gasped and smiled, like a child being presented with a new toy. He dropped Amanda and knelt down to scoop up the cat in his trunk-like arms. He cradled the animal and stroked it affectionately. "Oh you poor little kitty, are you lost? Awwww, aren't you cute?"

He stroked the cat gently, completely contradicting his fearsome looks. Amanda was a little surprised by this, but knew an opportunity to escape when she saw one. Whilst the man was distracted by the feline, she tiptoed away, praying he wouldn't notice.

"HEY! WHERE ARE YOU GOING?"

"Rats!" Amanda took to her heels.

The man lumbered after her, the cat in his arms.

She took a turn down a side street, pushing people and market traders away in succession.

The man thundered after her, barging anything in his way to one side. Many villagers made the wise choice to stand aside, so as to avoid being trampled by this behemoth.

Amanda glanced behind her. He was catching up to her fast. *How can someone that big be so fast?* she thought. "Hey," Amanda panted. "Can we talk about this?"

"Give me my refund!" he shouted after her.

Amanda had a feeling that she wasn't going to outrun this behemoth. Therefore, she only had one option. As much as she hated using her magic in public, it was the only way she was going to be able to escape. Amanda's hands turned aflame.

"Here I go!"

Amanda blasted the ground beneath her feet with fire. A powerful backdraft lifted her into the air. The flames behind her set alight the

Chapter 1

nearby market stalls. People screamed, scrambling for buckets of water whilst others tried to stamp the fire out.

"Sorry!" she called back at them. The flames carried her over the row of nearby buildings and into the next street. She hoped she could bide herself some time before the man caught up with her.

Amanda landed, sure that she had put some distance between her and the man. Her hands were still aflame, so she patted them against her skirt to put them out. Determined to outrun the big lug, she ran ahead—only to find herself at a dead end.

"Rats!"

The man caught up to the street Amanda had escaped to. She may have thought she could outsmart him by flying over, but he was native to Ashfeld and knew it well. This street led to a dead end—and he was sure to have Amanda caught in seconds.

"I've got you now!" However, when he turned into the dead end, Amanda wasn't there. It was as if she had disappeared into thin air. He overturned the boxes and barrels lining the side street to see if she could be hiding—but to no avail. The man scratched his chin, puzzled.

The cat, still in his grip, let out a small *meow*.

"Awww, are you hungry, Mr. Whiskers? Let's get you something to eat."

When she was sure he was gone, Amanda let go of the invisibility spell and the wall at her back. She breathed a sigh of relief and wiped her brow. *Close one.*

The walk back to her house felt longer, and she was empty handed. She dared not go back to the market to collect her things, and she didn't fancy giving a demonstration of her magical abilities again if the man showed up. So she cut her losses and headed home.

Maybe it won't be so bad—being homeless, Amanda thought. *I mean: no rent to pay. I can go wherever I want. What's not to like? But I may not have food, shelter or someplace warm. Oh, who cares!* When Amanda weighed her options, the idea didn't seem great. *I'm in trouble.*

As she turned the corner near her house, she spotted Kimerian soldiers striding down her street. She hid around the corner and out of sight. Kimerian soldiers were often bad news.

What are they doing here? They aren't after me, are they?

Maybe they had come to take her away after the blatant misuse of her powers. Though, she did wonder why they had never arrested her for it before. She carefully gazed round the corner, but the Kimerians did not seem interested in her. Instead, they nailed a picture to a nearby wall and carried on down the street.

When they were gone, Amanda crept out from her cover to examine the paper they'd left behind. It was a wanted poster, although she wondered why they would bother. This was a small town. She read it out of curiosity.

It showed a picture of what appeared to be a bear with wings. The notice underneath read:

Have you seen this birthmark? A child bearing this mark is missing. If found, please return him to Wrightson—where his family waits for his return. 250,000 gold coins reward for ~~capture~~ safe return.

It looked like the previous statement had been crossed out.

"Two hundred and fifty thousand?" Amanda practically gasped the number out. She had never seen a bounty that large before—even the worse criminals hardly warranted more than twenty thousand. Whoever this person was, someone was going through a lot of trouble to get them back. "What I wouldn't give for that kind of money. I'd be able to do anything. Including . . ." An idea crept into her mind. *"Pay off my rent."*

She shook her head. She wouldn't even know where to begin looking. Besides, it was long before nightfall and she had to collect ingredients for her potions.

Chapter 2

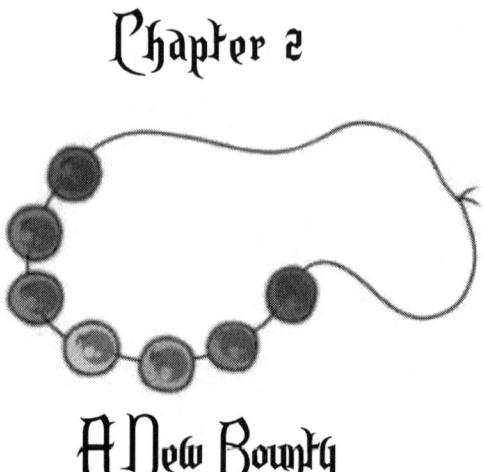

A New Bounty

Forest of Celt

Before night came, Amanda headed towards the forest to collect more ingredients for her potions. In the past—when she had money to do so—she would purchase them from people in the market. In fact, the market usually had far superior ingredients than what she could find in the forest—usually imported from Celtland's sister country Brittana. However, since her finances had dried up, she was somewhat limited to the stuff she could afford. Anything that she couldn't get she had to scrounge for in the forest. Unfortunately, with winter approaching, it meant that all the good ingredients were hard to come by.

After foraging for an hour, all she had to show for her efforts were a few toadstools, some flowers and a few bits of weeds. Nothing to help her make anything more glamorous than a light medicine—if that. Realising what a waste of time it had been, Amanda found a quiet spot in the forest and sat down to have a light meal. She unpacked her knapsack and helped herself to some pieces of bread. She ate it feeling somewhat forlorn, barely making any effort to chew or even swallow.

Why am I even bothering? she thought, realising that she was fighting a losing battle. *It doesn't matter how much money I make—I'll never be able to pay back Berger. Where did it all go wrong for me? Why can't it be back in the days where things were good. Happy...*

She sighed deeply. *I miss you, Wilfred.*

A rustle in the bushes caught her attention, but it passed and she dismissed it. As she was about to take another bite of her bread, there was another rustling sound. Amanda stopped and looked behind her. "Who's there?"

Just the wind, she thought. *Don't be so jumpy.*

Her attempt to take a bite of her bread was interrupted by yet another rustling. This one was much louder than before. Amanda dropped her food and jumped to her feet. "Hello?"

The bushes rustled very slightly, but there was no reply. But Amanda knew that someone was there—she could feel them watching her. "Hello?" she shouted, trying not to sound scared. "Is there anybody in there?"

Amanda was never very good at being confrontational. She never considered herself a fighter, despite being adept at magic. But she did know that when she needed to defend herself, she could at least try to sound scary.

"If you don't want to get hurt, you come out right now!"

No reply came from the bushes. Amanda held up one hand, setting it alight with fire. "I won't warn you again."

She gradually walked towards the bushes, holding out a flaming hand and moved carefully and slowly. "I'm warning you. I'm a sorceress and I'm not afraid to use magic!"

Amanda walked as close to the bushes as she dared, keeping her fire hand at bay. With her other free hand, she reached towards the bushes. "I'm going to count to three." She could feel her brow sweating and her teeth chattering. "One . . . two . . . three!"

She pulled back the foliage and launched her flaming hand outwards.

There was nothing behind it.

Chapter 2

She breathed a sigh of relief and dispelled the fire on her hand before she could do any damage. *Just stress making me hear things*, Amanda told herself. *Silly me.*

Her stomach rumbled and she remembered how hungry she was. She returned to her knapsack.

"HEY! You get your hands away from that!"

Amanda's hand lit up again when she saw someone digging into her knapsack. She held the fire towards the intruder, who cowered back, curling up in terror. "Please don't hurt me."

It was just a boy with golden hair. His clothes looked a little dirty and had a few tears in them in places. He tried to crawl away from her, still startled by her display of power. Amanda dispelled the fire once more and held up her hands as way of a parley. "Look, I'm not going to hurt you, okay? I just . . . what are you doing in my knapsack?"

"I was just hungry," the boy whined. "I'm sorry, I didn't mean to steal from you. I just lost my food."

The poor kid looked starved. His clothes were dirty and tattered and he barely looked like he was able to stand up. But then again, Amanda had heard stories of bandits using children as a trap to prey on unsuspecting travelers, so she was a little suspicious.

It was a pity that her psychokinetic magic didn't extend to telepathy—otherwise she could have learned in seconds whether he was genuine or not. "Okay, look," Amanda said, reaching into the knapsack. "If you want something to eat, you can have something.

Okay? But you shouldn't take things from people without asking. Here."

She threw the boy an apple, deciding not to give him the best food yet as she was still unsure what this kid's intentions were. The boy caught it and almost instantly devoured it. He certainly seemed hungry. "What are you doing out here anyway?" Amanda asked.

"Looking for my parents," the boy replied.

"Where are they?" Amanda asked.

"I don't know. They said that they'd follow after me, but I haven't seen them."

"Where do you live?"

"Watergate Pass."

"That's . . . about seven miles that way," Amanda said, pointing. "How did you get out here on your own?"

"I ran," the boy replied. He finished eating the apple, even the core. "What's your name?"

"Er, Amanda."

"Nice to meet you, Amanda. I'm Daryl."

"Yeah, hi."

"You . . . haven't seen my parents have you?"

"Er, no . . ."

"Oh," Daryl looked disappointed. "Could you help me find them? I'm lost and I don't know where they are."

"Oh, ah . . ." Amanda gritted her teeth. This was certainly something she didn't expect. "Er, listen, kid. I don't mean to be rude—but I . . . kinda have problems of my own at the moment. I don't really have the time to . . ."

"Oh . . ." Daryl looked downhearted. "Okay."

Amanda's conscience played on her. How could she leave this poor boy in the forest? "Er, listen. How about I take you into town? We can maybe ask if anyone has seen your parents there?"

"Really?" Daryl piped up. "That would be so nice of you."

"Yeah," Amanda said. She picked up her knapsack and bag of ingredients. "Come on, we'd best get up before night."

"Oh right!" Daryl cried overly excited. He jumped to his feet, almost like a completely different person. "Let's go."

He charged past Amanda, as if he knew the way already. "Hey, don't run off!"

"Come on!" Daryl cried, turning back to her. "I don't want to keep my parents waiting." He was acting like he had *already* found his

Chapter 2

parents, even though they were nowhere near town. "I'll be with them again in—AH!"

Daryl tripped on a loose rock and tumbled forward, hitting the grass with full force.

"I told you not to run off," Amanda sighed.

Daryl tried to get up, but couldn't stand. He sat down instead, putting both hands over a knee. He stammered a couple of times, then wailed loudly. His cries concerned Amanda somewhat, thinking it could draw attention to any predators that may be in the area. She quickly moved towards him.

"What's wrong?"

Daryl looked up, his eyes watering and his bottom lip quivering. "I have an ouchie."

Sighing hard, Amanda knelt down. "Let me have a look."

She rolled up his trouser leg slightly, causing Daryl to wince in pain. She noticed a red mark on his knee. Amanda moved her hands up and around his knee, but nothing felt broken. It was just a sprain.

"This should be easy enough to fix. Hold still, this may feel strange—but it won't hurt, I promise."

Amanda's hands glowed green as she held them over his knee. The green energy moved around Daryl's leg, slowly healing the damage and erasing the pain, like it never happened in the first place. Daryl rubbed his leg, surprised that he couldn't feel pain anymore. "How did you do that?" Daryl asked. "Are you . . . are you a magic user?"

"I prefer the term sorceress myself," Amanda replied.

"Wow!" Daryl gasped. "That is amazing!"

"Oh," Amanda said, catching something on his ankle, "you got a bit of a bruise down here as well."

She examined the bruise, only to discover that it actually wasn't a bruise. It was a mark. No. A birthmark. Amanda looked closer—it had a strange familiarity to it. Almost like a bear with wings.

Amanda recognised the mark—it was the same from the posters she saw in town. Her eyes widened in amazement. She had to blink to double check that she wasn't imagining things. No. It *was* the same mark as the one on the poster.

This . . . this is the boy.

She looked at Daryl, who looked back at her with a somewhat worried expression. "Are you okay?"

Amanda snapped back to reality. "Oh yes. I'm fine. Sorry, I just thought I saw something. But it's nothing."

Suddenly, an idea ran through Amanda's brain. This boy had the birthmark that was listed on the poster. It *had* to be him. That birthmark was too specific not to be. He was the one that everyone was looking for—and he had appeared right in her hands.

Amanda then remembered the reward for finding and returning him. 250,000 coins. A sly smile went across her face.

"You know—Daryl, was it? I want to apologise for being so rude to you earlier."

"It's okay," Daryl said.

"And you know, I think I *may* have seen your parents after all."

Amanda knew that she was being dishonest, but then desperate times called for desperate measures.

"Really?" Daryl asked, beaming. "You saw my parents?"

"Why sure, your parents are . . ."

"Glenda and Marcus."

"Glenda and Marcus, yeah. Sure I do. In fact I heard that they were heading to Wrightson. They told me they would meet you there."

"Really? They're alive?"

"Well, yes . . . why shouldn't they be?"

"Oh that is good! I was so worried for them."

"Don't worry," Amanda said. "Stick with me, I'll take you there. But first, let's get you somewhere warm, we'll head for Wrightson in the morning."

"Oh, Amanda, you're the best!"

"Think nothing of it. Now, you all right to walk?"

Daryl stood straight up. "Yes, ma'am."

"Follow me. It's just a little walk this way."

Daryl followed behind as Amanda headed back home. She tried to keep her smile from Daryl at all times. She could barely contain her excitement. All she had to do was return Daryl to his parents and 250,000 coins would be hers.

What could possibly go wrong? Amanda thought.

Although her home wasn't that far away, Daryl had made the journey feel longer than it should have been. Ever since discovering that Amanda was a sorceress, he couldn't stop asking questions. He had never met a real life sorceress before and wanted to know everything about it. *Everything.*

The problem was that he asked *too* many questions at once—more than Amanda could answer. And his constant talking was starting to give her a headache. Where was all this energy coming from? Maybe when Amanda used her healing magic she must have used a little too much and healed him to full health. And a child with full energy could be a handful at the best of times.

"And what does that gem do?" Daryl asked, pointing to the white one around her neck.

"Ice magic," Amanda replied, somewhat grumpily.

"Wow. And that orange one?"

"Fire."

Daryl winced a bit on hearing that. "And that green one?"

"Healing."

"What about that blue one?"

"Wind."

"And that orange one?"

"You just asked me that. Fire."

"Oh . . . and what about that . . . light blue one?"

"Hey, I got an idea! How about we play a game? See who can keep quiet the longest?"

"That game sounds boring."

"Yeah, the idea of the game is *not* to talk . . ." She rubbed her head, the throbbing inside her temple made it feel like her brain was about to explode from the inside.

"Can I ask a question?" Daryl piped up.

"What?"

"Can you control the weather with your magic?"

"No."

"Can you bring the dead back to life?"

"No . . ." *If only I could.*

"Oh . . . oh . . . I know! Can you use your magic to . . . to . . . turn lead into gold?"

"If I did, you think I'd be living the life that I am?"

"Oh . . . oh . . . can you, er . . . can you . . . oh, oh!"

"WHAT?" Amanda lost her temper, the incessant throbbing inside her head becoming too much. "Why are you asking so many questions? Why can't you just be silent for a few moments?!"

Daryl stopped and recoiled back, shrinking back from her with his fingers on both sides of his mouth. Amanda suddenly felt bad for shouting at him. "Look, I'm sorry, kid. I've just had a really bad time recently. I didn't mean to shout . . . maybe, maybe we could just . . . walk in silence for a bit."

Daryl's eyes became wet and he started sniffing. Now Amanda felt terrible. "No, really, I'm sorry, I didn't mean to snap."

"No, it's not that," Daryl said. "I need to go."

"Oh, okay . . . well then let's hurry on."

"No. I need to *go*."

"*Oh.*" Unfortunately there was not a lavatorium around for miles. "Well, can you hold it?"

"I . . . I . . ." He crossed his legs.

"Okay, okay, er . . . there's a bush you can use." Amanda pointed towards a nearby one.

Daryl carefully tiptoed over to the bush, taking hold of his suspenders. "You're not, going to watch me are you?" he asked Amanda. "I can't go if I'm being watched."

"Oh no, of course not." Amanda turned round and put her hands over her eyes. She actually enjoyed the few minutes of silence; it gave her head a chance to calm down. Who would have thought that a six-year-old could be such hard work?

Just think of the reward. Just think of the reward.

"You done?" Amanda asked after a few seconds. No reply. "Daryl? You done?" He didn't reply again. When he didn't reply to her a third time, she risked turning back, hoping that Daryl wasn't still doing his business.

Her eyes dropped and she let out a huge gasp when she saw that Daryl wasn't there. Her head went from side to side, but he was nowhere to be found.

"Daryl? Daryl?"

No, no, no. I can't lose the reward now!

She frantically started pulling back the bushes, trying to find him. "Come on, Daryl, this isn't funny!" Amanda moaned. "It will be dark soon. Come on, this is serious! This forest can be dangerous at night!"

A nearby bush rustled. Amanda almost cheered with relief; at least Daryl made it easy for her. She pulled back the bushes only to be greeted by two bright, blue eyes. "There you are! Come on now, let's get moving."

Chapter 2

The eyes glared at Amanda. "Come on Daryl, come out from there!"

"Come out from where?" Daryl asked, behind her.

"Oh give me strength," Amanda sighed, turning round. "Come out from there, we have to get back before ... how did you get there?"

"Where?"

"There."

"I was behind the bushes." He pointed behind him.

If Daryl's there ... then ... who is behind this ...

"Oh ... rats ..."

Amanda closed the bushes carefully, stood up and started backing away. "Daryl. I think we'd better move away, very ... very ... slowly."

"Why?"

"Just ... do as I say."

The bush near Amanda exploded, nearly knocking her flat on her back. A huge wolf leapt out and stood on all fours in attack position. Its fur was silver grey and its eyes blue as the sky. Its glinting jaws dripped with saliva as the beast snarled.

"What is that?" Amanda gasped, backing away towards Daryl.

"It's ... a moon wolf ... ," Daryl gasped, more with awe than fear. "I only read about them in books. I thought they were extinct."

The moon wolf held its ground, jaws gnashing. It let out a huge growl and fixed its eyes on Amanda and Daryl.

Amanda got to her feet. "You wanted to see how my magic works, I'll show you."

"Don't hurt it!" Daryl cried.

"Don't worry, I won't," Amanda promised, holding up her other hand. A cold blast of air formed around her palm. "I'll just freeze it where it stands. It'll thaw out after an hour—just enough for us to get away."

Amanda shot her arm forward towards the wolf, sending a small blizzard towards it. But the wolf dodged to one side to avoid the blast. Surprised at how fast it was, Amanda fired another blast of cold air towards it. The wolf dodged that as well, too fast for her spells. Amanda tried again, this time using both hands to cast the spell to create an arching blast of wind. The wolf scrambled up a tree, completely avoiding the cold wind. When it had passed, it jumped down, back into attack position.

"Wow," Daryl gasped. He had read about moon wolves being incredibly fast—but seeing it in action was another thing altogether.

"Ah," Amanda gasped. "Okay, new plan. RUN!"

Amanda and Daryl turned and ran in the opposite direction as fast as they could. The wolf followed in hot pursuit. No matter how fast Amanda and Daryl tried to escape, the wolf matched them step for step. After several seconds, it became clear that outrunning this wolf was going to be a problem.

"Okay," Amanda panted. "Looks like we'll have to do this the hard way." She prepared her fire magic. "Daryl, when I say the word, grab onto me. I'll get us out of—ARGH!"

She did not spot the root that sprung out of the ground (or so it seemed), catching Amanda by the foot in the same way that Daryl had been caught out earlier. She fell forward, landing face first on the ground. "Ow!"

No sooner had she tried to get up then she saw the shadow of the enormous wolf (nearly as big as she was) jumping on top of her with teeth bared. Amanda put her hands over her face as she waited for the wolf to bite down on her.

She waited. And waited. And waited. The bite never came. She allowed herself a look, opening one eye.

To her surprise, the wolf wasn't anywhere near her anymore. It had taken the knapsack and had its snout buried inside. The wolf pulled out a large cooked chicken and started to eat it.

"So that's why it was following us," Daryl said. "It was hungry."

Amanda watched as the wolf filled its belly, spitting out a bone. Amanda picked it up, looking at the bone with some disappointment. *I was saving that chicken*, she thought.

"Aww, aren't you a cute little doggie," Daryl cooed, hugging the animal and stroking its head. The wolf didn't seem to mind it—in fact it looked like it enjoyed the attention.

"Don't get too close to it," Amanda warned. She took Daryl by the hand and gently pulled him away from the wolf, knowing that the creature could turn any second. "Come on, let's get going."

"Can't we stay a little longer?" Daryl moaned as Amanda pulled him away.

"No we can't," Amanda sternly replied. "It's getting dark and we need to get you back home."

Whilst I still have a home to take him back to, Amanda thought.

A low whine came behind them. Amanda stopped and turned round. The wolf was behind them again, but this time it did not look like it was going to attack. Instead, it was sitting up, panting and tilting its head, looking more like a puppy dog.

"O . . . kay," Amanda said. She and Daryl took a few more steps. When she looked back, the wolf was behind them again, seemingly in the same position as before. "Okay, what gives?"

"I think he's following us," Daryl said.

"Oh no," Amanda shouted. "You are *not* coming home with us, mister! No way! Go on! Scram! Shoo! Go away!"

The wolf lowered its ears, raised its eyes and let out a pitiful whine.

"Aww, he just wants a friend," Daryl said, stroking the head of the creature again. "He's so cute. Can we keep him?"

"Don't you start," Amanda said.

"Please?" Daryl begged. "He's not dangerous. He was just hungry."

"No. Way!" Amanda replied sternly.

"Why not?" Daryl asked.

"Well, for one thing, I'm not allowed to have pets in my house. Secondly, I have too much stuff around my house that could be dangerous. Thirdly, in case you hadn't noticed—he's a *wolf!* And wolves aren't exactly household pets!"

"But . . . I want to keep him . . ." Daryl's eyes became wet and his bottom lip started quivering.

A New Bounty

"Oh no, no, no, don't do that," Amanda panicked. "Don't give me that look, please? Look, if . . . if you stop that I'll . . . I'll . . . I'll show you a magic trick! How's that? Come on, kid, work with me here!"

Daryl's eyes became so wet that the tears were about to burst forth any moment. His lip quivered like an earthquake as a cry rose up from his throat. Even the moon wolf was looking at her with big, sad eyes.

Amanda exhaled a deep sigh, defeated. "Fine! He can come home with us."

"Really?" Daryl cried, switching from sad to happy in an instant, as only a child could do. "Yay! Come on, Wolvie, you're coming to stay with me and Amanda."

"Wolvie?"

"That's what his name is," Daryl replied, stroking under Wolvie's chin.

Amanda eyed Wolvie as he passed by and pointed at him. "You just better be house trained." Wolvie responded by lifting up his tail and farting in her face. She rolled her eyes upwards. "Lovely . . ."

Amanda continued her walk home, coming back with three times the mouths to feed.

"Thanks for letting me take Wolvie, Amanda. You're the best."

"Don't mention it—seriously don't."

"Amanda?"

"Yes?"

"What does that light blue gem do?"

Amanda sighed hard. "Water magic."

"And that grey one?"

"Invisibility."

"And that big red one?"

"You don't want to know."

"And that blue one?"

"You already asked me! It's wind! WIND!"

"Oh . . . and that purple one?"

"Keep pushing me and you'll find out!"

The poster didn't specifically say "Dead or Alive," did it?

Chapter 3

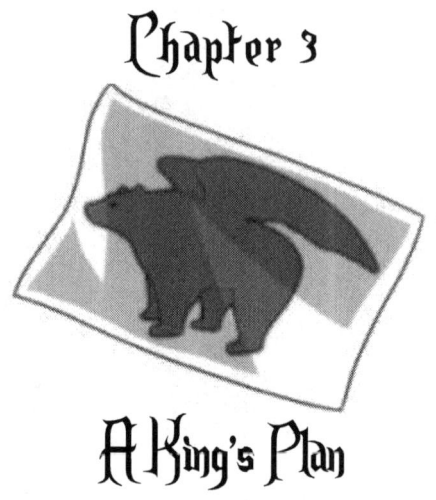

A King's Plan

Castle Gryphenpyre, Wrightson

Captain Luthar walked down the long corridors leading towards the throne room. The floor was decorated with red carpet and the walls were painted a golden colour. Hanging from the walls was picture after picture of King Kimera—each one about seven to eight feet in height, taking up as much space on the wall as it could. Luthar sighed to himself. He remembered when it was Queen Sheena's pictures on the walls—and she didn't have *nearly* the amount of pictures he did.

A couple of Kimera's guards at the end of the corridor saluted Luthar as he approached and opened the door into the throne room. The inside of this room was decorated in the same colour scheme as the corridor preceding it, except that it was even more of a shrine dedicated to Kimera than outside. There were several more pictures across the wall and even statues of him at every place there could be, made out of pure gold. Kimera's vanity was a very expensive hobby—expensive for the people of Wrightson that was!

Naturally, all the pictures and statues of Kimera depicted him as far more muscular than he was in reality, but that was only because Kimera had asked for it. One artist decided to go against this and paint him in the way he was in real life, and it was fair to say that he wasn't able to accept any more commissions, considering that one needed hands to paint.

Kimera lay across his golden throne, looking incredibly bored and yawning constantly. Near the foot of his throne, a couple of guards had forced a peasant to his knees whilst he pleaded his case to Kimera. However, it appeared that his pleas were going on deaf ears as Kimera did not look the least bit interested.

"Please, I beg you to show mercy, Your Majesty," the peasant pleaded. He was a gaunt, scrawny fellow that looked like he hadn't eaten in days. Luthar was amazed he could even talk altogether. "I was hungry—my . . . my family and I haven't eaten in days."

"So you thought it would be right to steal a loaf of bread?" Kimera asked, looking at his own reflection in the gem of his rings. "If you were so hungry, why not just buy it?"

Kimera almost sniggered at himself. He knew full well that this whelp could never afford a luxury like that. Not since he had imposed rations on the poorer classes of the city, just so that he could enjoy the finer things.

"My family and I can barely afford to pay for food like that," the peasant protested. "The rations we are granted aren't enough to feed us . . ."

"Wait," the King said, sitting up. "Are you saying that the rations that *I* provide you aren't enough?"

He stood up and walked down towards the man, scowling at him. "It sounds to me that you are being ungrateful. After everything I provided for you, you *still* want more. You stole bread, bread that I provided my people. And if you steal from my people . . ." He got up close into the man's face. ". . . you steal from ME!"

Kimera was looking forward to glowering before the begging peasants, but suddenly, the peasant seemed to lose all fear. "Steal from you? *You're* the one that steals from *us*! We're starving in the streets and you do nothing to help us! When the real King returns, I hope he throws you to the wolves!"

Chapter 3

"Real . . . King?" Kimera asked. "What are you talking about? *I'm* your real King!"

"I mean the *true* King!" the peasant cried, getting to his feet. "We've all heard the news about the real King. Son of Queen Sheena—"

The man was forced back to his knees with a punch to his stomach. But the man's defiance had angered Kimera and he was not prepared to let that go unpunished.

"Had you not opened your mouth, I may have spared you a little longer," Kimera snarled. "It's time you all learned how we maintain order around here. Guards, have that man hung!"

"Hanged, Your Majesty."

Kimera turned towards the guard that spoke. "I beg your pardon?"

"The term is 'hanged,' Your Majesty," the guard continued. His comrade shook his head and mouthed "no," but the guard didn't seem to notice.

Kimera narrowed his eyes and walked slowly towards the guard. "Well, thank you for that correction. Seeing as you are apparently versed in the ways of words, perhaps you could correct me on this statement." He cleared his throat. "'The guard was *hanged* for his insolence.' Am I saying that right? Was the insolent guard *hanged?*"

The guard started to sweat. "My apologies, Your Majesty! He'll be hung as you requested!"

"Good," Kimera sneered. "Now get him out of my sight."

The peasant was dragged from the throne room, screaming defiantly with all his lungs. His screams could be heard down the corridor even as the doors slammed shut.

"I do enjoy meeting with the lower classes," Kimera chuckled. "Nothing makes me feel better than putting them in their place—out of my sight! Ah, Luthar—please do come forth."

Luthar felt sick to his stomach over the way Kimera handled that situation. This would never have happened under the rule of Queen Sheena. She treated her people with respect, Kimera treated his people like cattle. He stepped forward as commanded.

"So, I assume you are here to tell me the good news?" Kimera asked, rubbing his hands. "That we have the boy in our custody?"

"Not yet, Your Majesty," Luthar replied. "But we have guards all around the country searching for him."

A King's Plan

Kimera slumped back, letting out a deflated grunt. He had hoped for better news. "What about the bounty—I mean, appeal—I put out?"

"We have posters out all across the major cities, Sire," Luthar replied.

"But has anyone come forward yet?"

"Well, no, Sire. We've only just put them out. These things take time . . ."

"Time?" Kimera screeched. "You *do* realise the importance of finding this boy, right?"

"Of course, Sire."

"Then you know that *time* is not something we have! Word is already starting to spread about the boy! How could this happen? Weren't you supposed to contain it?"

"I know not, Your Majesty."

Luthar still had no idea how Kimera came by this information about Daryl—but whoever his source was, they were spot on. Now, rumours of Queen Sheena's offspring were starting to circle around Wrightson. As such, Kimera had imposed an embargo on the city to keep the people in. No one was allowed in or out and visitors to the city were regulated very strictly.

"I can't have my people talk about me behind my back!" Kimera moaned. "I've sacrificed too much to let this fall through."

"You mean like how you sacrificed your sister?"

Kimera turned to Luthar, amazed at his defiance. "Luthar . . . are you accusing your King of having something to do with Queen Sheena's death? That's a pretty big accusation . . . I assume that you have proof of this?"

Luthar took a breath, paused, then exhaled it in a defeated sigh.

"I thought not. So I will let this insult go this one time."

He turned away from Luthar again—though the reminder of the day his sister met an end brought a smile to his face.

"Now, Luthar, I believe you have a child to find. And do not even *think* of coming anywhere near me unless you have good news."

"With respect, Sire. It was *you* that summoned me!"

Kimera scowled again. "Fine, just get out of my sight."

Luthar was only too happy to leave. "Your Majesty . . . you promise that no harm will come to the boy when he's returned?"

Kimera seemed more interested in his own fingernails than in answering Luthar's question. "If I say yes, will you fall in line?"

Chapter 3

"I will, Your Majesty."

"Very well," Kimera replied. "The boy will not be harmed. Now you can leave."

Luthar did not look back, his stomach feeling like it was being eaten away by poison. He despised this man so much—and despised it even more that he had to obey his every command. This man whom had wounded him more deeply than any blade ever could.

Still, at least he promised not to harm Daryl. That was something at least. Assuming he kept his word.

"Don't let anyone disturb me," Kimera ordered the guard stationed outside his bedchamber. The guard nodded and stood nearby the door as Kimera closed it behind him. He decided to retire for the night, feeling exhausted from all this worry. He just prayed that Daryl would be found soon. Being King was everything he ever dreamed of. He would not let it slip away. As long as Daryl was out there, his role was in jeopardy.

He felt a headache coming along and grabbed the side of his temple, the inside of his skull pounding like the beat of a drum. *A little wine will ease this.* He wandered to the table at the end of the bedroom, picking up the diamond encrusted jug filled with Golden Sun, the best wine in the Southern Lands. He took a golden wine goblet and poured the orange tinted liquid into the goblet.

"That is not a good deterrent for pain."

Kimera jumped out of his skin, dropping the jug. The wine spilled out as the container hit the ground, most of it splashing out with the initial impact, the rest slowly seeping through the funnel onto the ivory-coloured carpet.

Someone was sitting on his bed—but Kimera was sure that he did not see him there before. He was dressed all in black with a heavy overcoat and a large fedora. Over one side of his face was a white half-mask with lines drawn on either side. He sat crossed legged, a large, black tome resting on it, his gloved hand turning the dirty yellow pages. "The alcohol does not make your agony go away, it only conceals it." He spoke slowly and quietly, taking his time with his words like he would not be rushed. His voice seemed to carry no emotion and chilled Kimera to the bones with each word he spoke. "It hides you from the true agony that you hold within your soul."

"You!" Kimera gasped.

"You want to lock your door," the man in black suggested. "That is unless you intend for your servants to know your dark little secrets."

Taking this advice, Kimera locked the door with a key from the bedside table.

"You have a question that you wish to ask," the man in black said, remaining seated. "Ask it and I may have an answer."

"You told me that Daryl was at that village," Kimera snapped at him.

"And that was not an untruth," the man in black replied. "Impatience was your enemy here."

Kimera could barely understand what this man said half the time—speaking to him was like trying to decipher a puzzle that was harder to crack than it needed to be. "Are you saying that this is *my* fault that Daryl got away?"

"If that is the intent that you take from my words."

Kimera wished this man talked in normal Commonspeak and not in riddles. "You're supposed to be helping me!" Kimera shouted, then realised he should keep his voice down.

"Have I not?" the man in black asked. "Who was it that came to you in your time of need?"

Kimera remembered that day well, just over six years ago. He was in a tavern, drinking himself into a stupor to overcome his depression. He had become deeply resentful of being second fiddle to his sister, the Queen. What had she really done to deserve it?

Chapter 3

Kimera had fought in wars for Celtland (that was before he let himself go a little), he had all the skills to lead Celtland. But Father had chosen Sheena as his successor—and that did not sit well with him at all.

He met with the man in black when he was trying to buy another round but had run out of money. He brought Kimera a drink and sat and talked with him. Kimera told him his story and his anxieties, even breaking down into tears at one point. The man in black listened to his story and seemed to take pity. The man in black offered him a chance to take everything he wanted and said that he would help him. It was because of him that Kimera was able to put a plan into action whereby he would become King and finally put an end to his sister once and for all.

The man in black stood up, his stature was so large that he dwarfed Kimera. "I assume you know the importance of finding this child?" he asked him.

"Of course I do," Kimera snapped. "With him out there, my claim to the throne is threatened."

"The importance of your claim is non-existent," the man said

"Non-existent?" Kimera screeched. "Are you saying me being King isn't important?"

With his head focused on the pages of his book, the man walked past Kimera, towards the door.

"Don't you turn your back on me!" Kimera shouted. "I am King; you will answer me!"

The man stopped and pointed two fingers towards his throat. Kimera suddenly felt his throat tighten, as if someone had put a noose around his neck.

"A King is only a title," the man said. "And words are only as powerful as those who speak them."

Kimera flew through the air as if picked up by an unseen force. He landed on his backside, his head near the spilled wine.

"If you follow the path of blood, blood will follow you."

Kimera sat up, one hand rubbing his head, the other clutching his throat. "What are you blabbering about?" he grumbled.

But the man in black was not there. He had vanished. Kimera never even heard the door being opened. Stumbling to his feet—and nearly tripping over his own weight—he bolted towards the door, only to find it still locked. *Impossible! He can't have walked through it.*

Rushing to his bedside table, he grabbed the key to unlock his door, throwing it open.

But all he saw was an empty corridor. It was like the man never existed in the first place. Kimera rubbed his aching head, his headache returning.

"Your Majesty?"

The guard eyed Kimera, rather befuddled. Kimera looked back at him with a blank expression. Then, remembering his role, he asked the guard in a demanding tone, "Did you see a man in black pass by here?"

"I did not, Your Majesty," the guard replied.

"Agh, never mind."

The guard looked into Kimera's quarters, noticing the spilled wine. "Your Majesty, is everything all right?"

"Everything is fine," Kimera snapped. "I . . . just had an accident with the wine jug."

"Shall I . . . get you more wine, Sire?" the guard asked, confused but not wanting to upset the King, seeing he was in distress.

"No!" Kimera snapped. "I mean, yes . . . get me some more wine!"

He slammed the door shut, leaning against it and rubbing his throbbing temple. His heart was racing at a million times a second. The man in black couldn't have just disappeared into thin air like that. It wasn't possible.

Was it?

Chapter 4

Home

Ashfeld

Amanda opened the door to her house and quickly ushered Daryl and Wolvie in, hoping no one would see them—especially not Berger. She closed the door and locked it.

"Wow! Is this your house?" Daryl gasped. His house had been relatively small compared to this one.

"Yeah, this is me," Amanda said.

"You have books here?" Daryl gasped, noticing the bookshelf next to Amanda's table. "Are these . . . spell books?"

"Some of them," Amanda replied, putting down her bag of ingredients near the table.

"Wow!" Daryl cried. He grabbed one and started to read. "I've never seen a spell book before." After skimming through it, he pulled out several more, dropping them on the floor.

"Hey! Careful!" Amanda shouted. She rushed over. But Daryl had already littered the floor with her books. "Oh! I had these in order!"

"Oh. What are these?" By the bookcase was a set of spherical glass objects, in a variation of different colours and with strange hieroglyphics. "Are these juggling balls?" Daryl picked a few of them up and threw them up in the air, trying to catch them.

"Hey, careful with those!" Amanda cried, remembering that those glass balls were presents brought back from a holiday in Hussana, when they visited the Pharoh's tombs. "They're precious and they—"

Break easily was what Amanda was going to say. But Daryl found that out the hard way as he fumbled to catch them and they slipped from his palms. The spheres shattered with little impact the moment they struck the floor. She angrily grabbed Daryl's wrist before he could take any more from the shelf.

"Quit. Breaking. My balls," she said very matter-of-factly.

"You put me off," Daryl complained.

She saw Wolvie jump onto her table, sniffing a green mixture in a bottle. "Ahhhh, keep away from that!" She tried to pull Wolvie off the table, which was quite difficult due to his large size. "That mixture isn't complete!"

Whilst Amanda struggled to keep Wolvie away from her table, Daryl perused the potions that she had on a nearby shelf. "Are these all magical potions?" Daryl asked.

"Not exactly," Amanda panted. "But a lot of the ingredients that make them are very rare—so don't break anything."

Wolvie began licking Amanda's face affectionately.

"Hey, cut that out!"

"What does this potion do?" Daryl asked, reaching for a red mixture.

"Keep away from that one!" Amanda shouted back, desperately trying to get Wolvie off her. "That one's dangerous!"

"Dangerous? How?"

"Dangerous as in 'if it gets in your eyes, they melt' dangerous! Will you just get off me!"

But Wolvie didn't seem to want to get off her.

"Aww, he's just playing," Daryl said. He then saw a sparkly blue-coloured potion in a large bottle. "Oooh, this is pretty," Daryl mused, picking it up. "What's inside this?" He tried to remove the stopper, but it was sealed tight.

Chapter 4

"Will you just get off me?" Amanda snapped at Wolvie, her face becoming wet with his saliva. "Okay, that's enough!"

She pushed Wolvie off her with as much strength she could muster in her arms, grunting forcibly. She then used her sleeve to dry herself. "Ewww, I'm all icky!" She turned to Daryl, who was still trying, unsuccessfully, to remove the stopper from the potion bottle. "HEY! PUT THAT—"

Daryl pulled the stopper off and fell back, the bottle flying out of his hands. It spun round a few times and then crashed, smashing to hundreds of pieces. Amanda's look of shock turned to a look of horror before turning annoyed. She plodded along to the blue puddle, already starting to soak into the floorboards. In seconds, the potion disappeared, like it was never there in the first place.

"Sorry," Daryl apologised.

"It's fine," Amanda sighed. "I'll make another one. Oh no, wait. I can't. Because the ingredients DON'T EXIST ANYMORE!"

"You're . . . not angry, are you?"

"Look, why don't you just stand over there and be quiet!" Amanda snapped, pointing to the corner of the room. Daryl, feeling a little bit guilty, did as he was told whilst Amanda stomped across the room. Her shoulders were raised and her fists clenched, the sides of her lips slightly curled. To Daryl, she almost reminded him of the jotuns of legend—giants who were said to be bad tempered and easily angered. Amanda picked up a broom and swept the glass away, muttering to herself.

Wolvie wandered over to Daryl. He rubbed his nose against him, panting gently. Daryl stroked the side of his head. "Ooh, aren't you a good little doggie?"

Wolvie panted and whined gently, rubbing his nose against him.

Daryl noticed a tiny mushroom on the floor that had rolled out from Amanda's ingredient bag. He picked it up and held it in front of Wolvie's nose. "Hey, you want to play catch, Wolvie?"

Wolvie nodded and let out a gentle growl.

"Catch!"

Daryl threw the mushroom through the air. Wolvie followed it and caught it in his mouth, bringing it back to Daryl. "Good boy, Wolvie!" They did this a few more times, throwing the mushroom farther each time.

Home

"You better not be up to anything back there," Amanda warned, sweeping the pieces of glass out her front door, hearing Wolvie's nails scraping against the floorboards.

"We're just playing," Daryl said. "Hey, Wolvie. Go long!"

This time Daryl threw the mushroom across the room, but he put in more force into this throw and Wolvie had to travel farther to try and catch it. He jumped and caught it in his mouth, but as he landed, he slid across the floor, towards a door to another room. Wolvie crashed into it and the door burst open. "Wolvie!" Daryl cried, running after him.

Amanda turned round and looked in horror when she saw where they were running to. "NO! DON'T GO IN THAT ROOM!"

Daryl ignored her and ran in. "You okay, Wolvie?"

He was a little surprised at what they found inside this new room. There was very little lighting here and the air was thick with dust, causing Daryl to cough a bit. In the middle of the room was a large, handmade cot, thick with cobwebs.

Amanda suddenly burst into the room. "Get out! Get out of here now!"

"Is that . . . a cot?" Daryl asked. "You have children here?"

"No I don't!" Amanda snapped. She tried to force Daryl and Wolvie out of the room, but Daryl didn't seem to want to move.

"Oh, is that you in that picture?"

Near the cot was a painting, also covered in dust and cobwebs. Daryl could see it was Amanda on one side—on the other side was a handsome man with short brown hair, clean shaven and with beautiful blue eyes, dressed in a cream shirt and blue trousers, a red scarf around his neck. In the picture he had his arm around her, and Amanda had her hand on his shoulder. Her belly was sticking out quite considerably—but this was not due to her being fat. They were both smiling.

"Who's that man?"

"No one, just get out!"

Amanda forced Daryl and Wolvie out of the room and slammed the door shut. "Who was that man?" Daryl asked. "Is he your boyfriend?"

"He's no one, just leave it, okay?" Amanda snapped.

"Well then why is he in the picture with you? And how come you're so big in that picture?"

Chapter 4

"Why do you have to ask so many questions?" Amanda furiously shouted. "Can't you just shut up for one second? Is that too much to ask?"

Daryl was stunned into silence. He looked down at the floor, his lip quivering. "I'm sorry . . . ," he stammered. "I . . . I didn't mean to be bad . . ."

"Oh," Amanda sighed, feeling bad. "Look, you're not bad. It's just . . . some things you need to be careful of. Some things can be . . . touchy for people. You understand?"

Daryl wiped his eyes. "I guess so."

Amanda felt like a witch. It wasn't his fault that he was curious, he was just a kid after all. It was in their nature to be curious at that age. "Look, how about I run you a bath and fix your clothes? Then I can cook you dinner. How's that?"

Whilst Daryl had his bath, Amanda washed and fixed his clothes. They were pretty torn and messed up, but Amanda was sure that she could fix them. And considering she didn't have any other clothes for Daryl to wear, she thought it would be best to get them cleaned up.

The good thing about having magic was that it meant she could do several things at once without getting her hands dirty. She got a pail, used her magic to create water to fill it, mixed in some soap and heated the water slightly. She then used her psychokinesis to dip the clothes in the water and gave them a quick wash and a scrub before drying them with a gentle heat of fire. Afterwards, she sewed them up until all tears were fixed. Thanks to her magic, what should have taken hours only took a few minutes.

When she was done, she folded them up nicely, put them in a basket and knocked on the lavatorium door. "Daryl, it's me. I got your clothes ready."

"It's open."

Amanda walked in carefully, holding the basket. "Everything okay?"

She was surprised to see both Daryl *and* Wolvie in the bath. Daryl was scrubbing Wolvie behind his ears, which the animal didn't seem to mind.

"Wolvie smelt a bit funny," Daryl said. "I thought we could give him a bath as well as there was space for both of us."

Home

Well, fair enough I guess, Amanda thought. "I, er, fixed your clothes. They're here, good as new."

"Thanks, Amanda. You're very kind."

"I'll, er . . . leave you to it."

She put the basket near the side of the door, near the towels. Wolvie crawled out of the bath, his fur holding most of the water as it dripped off him. "Oh, Wolvie!" Amanda moaned. "You got water all over the floor! This is going to make the wood rot. What have you got to say for yourself?"

Wolvie responded by shaking. All the water that was on him splashed across the whole room, soaking everything—including Amanda.

Daryl laughed as Amanda stood where she was, eyeing Wolvie grumpily. "I hate you," she whispered.

Wolvie just replied with a whimper and looked at her with puppy dog eyes.

Daryl and Wolvie cleared up and met Amanda in the dining room. Daryl's clothes looked much cleaner now and he even smelt like a rose. The bath had done him a world of good. Amanda was standing over a pot, mixing it with a spoon as it cooked over a fire. She put in a couple more shakes of salt into the mix before she heard Daryl come in.

"Hey, Daryl, you better?"

"Yeah, me and Wolvie are as clean as a whistle now," Daryl replied. He sniffed the air. "Oh, what's that?"

"I hope you're happy with beef stew," Amanda said. "I didn't have a lot of food left in the larder, but enough to make this at least."

"Oooh, my mum makes beef stew."

Wolvie licked his lips in anticipation as well.

"Well that's good," Amanda said. She lifted the spoon out to test it, but the stew tasted a little tepid. "Mmmmm, maybe it could be a little hotter."

Amanda held her hand near the flame and used a little bit of fire magic to raise it a bit higher. The flame underneath became stronger and fiercer and almost exploded with the power Amanda put into it.

Daryl saw the rising flame and he was taken back to his village. The rising heat, the fire licking around the buildings, the screams of the people trapped inside the roaring inferno. The image was fixed in his mind, implanted within his dreams—his nightmares. As the fire rose at the bottom of the pot, it looked like it was reaching out towards him beckoning him closer—luring him with the false promise of a warm embrace, when really it promised nothing but a burning death.

Daryl screamed and ran underneath the dinner table, causing Amanda to jump and turn round.

"Hey, what's going on?"

She looked underneath the table. Daryl was curled up at the end, his knees pressed up against his chest and rocking back and forth, letting out short, sharp breaths.

"Hey, you okay?" Amanda asked.

Daryl looked up upon hearing Amanda's voice. He scrambled from underneath the table and threw his arms around her, squeezing her so tight that he almost cut off her circulation. Amanda was a little taken aback by this and didn't understand where this came from. "Er, hey," she said nervously. "It's all right. It's okay . . ."

She hugged him back, but wasn't sure why he broke down like that. *I wonder what could have happened in his village.*

Despite his earlier episode, dinner passed without a hitch. It was now time for bed. She gave him the spare room next to her bedroom so that she could keep as close an eye on him as possible. She pulled the blanket over him, making sure he was tucked in comfortably. "Well, it's been fun," Amanda said, "but I think it's time to get some sleep."

"But I'm not tired," Daryl said.

"I am," Amanda yawned. "It's been a long day and I could really use some rest. Night, kid."

"Amanda?" Daryl asked.

"Can the questions wait until tomorrow? I'm really tired . . ."

"When are we going to meet my parents?"

"Soon," Amanda replied. "We'll go out to meet them tomorrow."

"Tomorrow? You promise me?"

"Sure thing."

"Oh wow! I can't wait to see them again."

"Neither can they. Well, goodnight . . ." She turned to leave the room.

"Amanda?"

Amanda stopped. "Yes?"

"You're a very kind person, you know that?"

"Well, thanks . . . that's very sweet of you."

"It's true. You've been so kind to me, offering to take me to my parents and letting me keep Wolvie."

"Don't mention it."

"Hey!" Daryl suddenly said. "Maybe you can come to stay with me and my parents when we meet them. I'm sure my parents wouldn't mind."

"That's . . . probably not a good idea."

"Why not? You could help my mum and dad with your magic."

"Yeah, see . . . people who practice magic aren't exactly . . . well . . . tolerated as much as they used to be."

"Can I at least ask them? I'm sure they will be happy with it. Then you won't have to be lonely anymore."

"Lonely?" That took Amanda by surprise. "I'm not . . . lonely."

"You live alone, don't you? So, you must be lonely."

Amanda had no answer to that. "I . . . guess . . ."

"Amanda," Daryl then asked. "Who was that person in the picture?"

"Look, kid," Amanda replied, somewhat irritated. "I told you I don't like to talk about it."

"Why? Was he a bad person?"

Amanda sighed long and hard. "No. He wasn't. In fact, he was perfect."

"Then, why don't you like to talk about it?"

Amanda sat on the chair besides Daryl's bed, somewhat morose. "I did something bad. And he left me."

"What did you do?"

"I don't really like to talk about it."

"Can't you tell him you're sorry?"

"I'd love to." Amanda closed her eyes. "But I haven't seen him in a year."

Daryl felt so sorry for Amanda, she looked so sad. It also made him sad to see her like this. "My mum always says things have a way of working themselves out," Daryl said. "Maybe . . . if he saw what a good person you are he would come back."

"You . . . ," Amanda hesitated. "You think I'm a good person?"

"Course I do," Daryl replied. "You're one of the nicest people I've ever met."

"You've only known me less than a day."

Chapter 4

"Yeah, but I can always see the good in people," Daryl replied. "And I can see that you're a nice person—you wouldn't have taken me in otherwise."

Amanda smiled. It had been a while since anyone had been this nice to her. In fact, it had been a while since *anyone* had been nice to her. "Thanks, Daryl." She stood up. "You get a good night's sleep."

"Amanda?"

"Yes?"

"Would you read me a bedtime story?"

"Maybe another day . . ."

"Please?"

Amanda sighed; though she took such a deep breath it came out more like a roar. "Fine!"

She wandered to the shelf, running a finger across the spines of the books she had. These were not spell books, but rather a collection of novels. She looked for one of the more child-friendly stories and pulled one out at random. "What about this one? *The Ice Maiden?* Many say this is the best story ever written."

"What's it about?"

"It's about this woman who gains ice powers and uses them to freeze all of Brittana. Only true love brings her back. I hear it's loosely based on the life of Zarracka Dragonkin."

"That sounds boring," Daryl whined. "Who'd really want to read that?"

"Yeah, I actually can't argue with you there," Amanda said. "It's okay I guess, but nowhere near as good as people say it is. And between you and me, I think the talking snow ghul in it is annoying as hell!" She replaced the book. "Well what kind of story *do* you want?"

"Something with knights and . . . and ghuls . . ."

Amanda scanned the spines of the books, picking one out and looking at the cover. "This one has a picture of a knight."

Daryl nodded. Amanda took her place next to Daryl and then began to read.

"And so, the Princess married the handsome Lord, who had risked everything to save her from the evil ghul. They married and lived happily ever after, until the end of their days."

Amanda closed the book, pouting. "What chauvinistic drivel! Even in this day and age these modern writers *still* think the 'Damsel in Distress' story is good writing. You never get a strong, female character that has to save the Prince—oh no, that would be *too* radical for these writers!"

Amanda decided that from here on she wouldn't choose a book solely based on the cover. People had always advised her against it anyway, but she never listened.

She chanced a look at Daryl, who was now fast asleep. Finally, Amanda could leave.

Who'd have thought looking after a six-year-old could be such a chore.

She nearly tripped over Wolvie on the landing, who was curled up by the stairs. Why he had picked this spot to sleep at she had no idea. *I guess animals are just better at picking awkward spots to sleep in.*

Amanda practically fell onto her bed upon entering her room, her head landing on the pillow. She felt like she could just drift away. It had been a long day today.

Well, at least all my problems will soon be at an end. Tomorrow, I'll take Daryl to Wrightson, pick up my reward and I can pay off Berger. And I'll have plenty of money to get my business up and running again.

"Daryl sure is sweet to tell me those things though."

Remember, you're just using him for the reward.

Yeah, I know.

"But . . . he was so nice to me."

Amanda opened her eyes, as if surprised by herself. Turning around onto her back, she slapped her face. "Get a grip! You're not his mother. You need the money, you want to be homeless?"

Amanda let out a huge sigh, then fatigue took hold of her once more. She turned to her side to blow out the candle by her bedside table, then she began to drift off into a deep sleep.

Just remember you're only doing this for the reward. You're not Daryl's mother.

You need the money.

You need the money.

But he was so kind . . .

No, don't even think about it. You're doing this for the money.

Nothing else.

Chapter 5

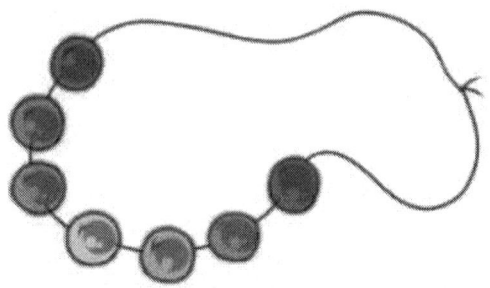

Terrible Loss

Ashfeld, Three Years Ago

Berger opened up the door to the house to show her possible tenants in. She had made sure that the house was especially tidy beforehand—these two looked like they were rich and she wanted to make a good impression.

"It may be quaint, but it's a nice little house," Berger said, leading them in. "This is the main hall, which is nice and spacious as you can see. You have a couple of extra rooms here and here, and upstairs can serve as a bedroom and a spare room if need be."

Wilfred and Amanda were all smiles as they walked in. "This is beautiful," Amanda said, feeling the wood of the house. "They even smell wonderful."

"Made from real ashwood," Berger said. "The smell gives it a nice relaxing feel I think."

"It certainly does," Wilfred said.

"So, if I may ask, My Lord," Berger said.

"How did you know I was a Lord?" Wilfred asked.

"Oh, I know a Lord when I see one," Berger replied. "Your stance alone tells me of your high birth."

"Yeah, but you don't have to call me Lord," Wilfred said. "I'm just the same as anyone else."

Berger was somewhat amazed at how humble Wilfred was. She had never met a Lord like him before. "Well, what brings you to our town of Ashfeld? We don't see many of your kind in our humble town."

"Peace and quiet mainly," Wilfred replied. "City life can be too hectic sometimes—you just want to settle down and relax."

Amanda wandered around, taking in the smell and feel of the house. "I love it," she gasped.

"Well, your wife certainly has taken to it," Berger commented.

"Oh, we're not married," Wilfred said. "Not yet anyway."

"Oh, my apologies . . ."

"Not at all. Amanda really wants to start up her own business and would like to be close to the forest to get her ingredients."

"Oh, what kind of business is she into?"

"Alchemy," Wilfred replied. "She trained at Valenco University and wants to start up her potion business."

"Oh, that sounds nice," Berger said. "Well, this place is a perfect spot as the market is only a few minutes' walk away."

Amanda was standing by a large open area in the house. "This place is perfect for my work table!" Amanda cheered. "And I can have the bookcase here, drawers for my ingredients here. It's perfect."

Wilfred and Amanda's gaze caught. They didn't say a word, but Wilfred could see from Amanda's look of excitement that she wanted this place badly. "We'll take it."

"You will?" Berger gasped, surprised. "Great! Rent is 150 coins a month. Just a couple of minor rules: any damages to the house you pay for and I have a strict no-pets policy. I normally ask that the tenants pay at least three months in advance to prove that they are genuine."

"Of course," Wilfred agreed. He took a bag from his belt and undid the tie. "Will this do?" He took a few of the contents— shining rocks that sparkled in the light.

"Are . . . ," Berger gasped. "Are these real diamonds?"

Chapter 5

"My father owns a diamond mine," Wilfred replied. "He let me have a few as an investment for the house. Here."

He gave the bag over to Berger, who then looked through it like a dog looking for food. When she pulled her head up from the bag, the smile on her face looked like it would take years to remove. It would actually be the last time that Amanda remembered Berger smiling. "Sir, madam . . . consider your rent paid for—for the next three years!" She then ran out, cheering ecstatically.

Wilfred took Amanda into his arms and they kissed passionately. "Thank you so much for this," Amanda said.

"This is just the start," Wilfred told her. "A whole new life begins for us now."

Amanda never knew how she got so lucky with Wilfred. He was a perfect boyfriend—so supportive and protective of her. She couldn't think of a better person to spend her life with.

They moved in less than a day and it didn't take long before they settled into their new life. Wilfred chipped in to help Amanda with the business, everything from buying her ingredients to helping her mix. He even found a use for his skills as a woodcutter, building the cart she used to transport her potions to the market. They may not have made a huge amount of money from the business, but everything they gained was profit, considering that Wilfred had now paid for their living for three years.

A year later, Amanda discovered that she was pregnant—and she and Wilfred could not have been happier. Wilfred was so excited that he even built a cot for the baby in one of the spare rooms. Amanda kept on with her potion business up until the baby was due, not wanting to sit around. About a month before the due date, Wilfred commissioned an artist to paint a picture of him and Amanda as they wanted to capture the happiness that this baby would bring them. They hadn't had a picture of them before, so Wilfred thought this would be the perfect opportunity.

It was less than a week for the supposed due date and Wilfred returned to Ashfeld from his trek in the Forest of Celt, having gone to get new ingredients for Amanda's potion. At least that's what he told her. In fact, he had gone back home to pick up a "special" package.

He checked the small bag that he carried over his shoulder, making sure the package was safely tucked away against all the toadstools, weeds and other things he had purchased. Amongst them was a tiny leather box containing Amanda's present. He had called in an old favour for some friends and they had prepared a special ring for her—a ring made from the purest diamonds imaginable.

Wilfred couldn't wait to show it to her and he could only imagine the look she would give him when he produced it to her. With a child on the way, he figured it was time to do the honourable thing. He only wondered why he hadn't done it sooner.

Barely able to contain his smile, he threw open the door to his house. "Amanda . . . ," he called out. "I'm back. Found some really good toadstools that you can use for . . ."

Inside, he saw Miss Berger standing with three women in gray cloaks. Berger turned round. "Wilfred," she said. "We wondered where you were."

"Miss Berger? What happened?"

The women didn't even want to look Wilfred in the eye. Berger took it upon herself to tell him the news. "It's Amanda. She collapsed. I brought her back here and called the nurses to her home . . . but . . ."

"What . . . what do you mean?" Wilfred asked. "Is she okay?"

The nurses showed themselves out, having done their duty. "You'll be in our prayers," one of them said as they passed. Wilfred noticed that she was carrying a set of bloody blankets.

"What's going on?" Wilfred asked, panic in his voice. "Is . . . is Amanda okay?"

"Amanda is fine," Berger replied, forlorn. She put a hand on Wilfred's shoulders. "But there were . . . complications . . ."

Wilfred turned back to the nurses as they left, catching the one with the bloody blankets again. His throat constricted. "No . . ."

"She's in there," Berger replied, looking towards the spare room. "She hasn't come out in a while." With teary eyes, she looked back at Wilfred one last time. "I'll leave you two alone."

Berger left before her tears could burst forth. Ice gripping his veins, Wilfred dropped the bag of ingredients and then walked towards the spare room. The door creaked painfully as he pushed it open. "Amanda?"

Amanda was standing over the cot, her hands resting on the side of it. She didn't respond as Wilfred walked in—almost as if she was

Chapter 5

ashamed to look at him. Wilfred moved closer to her, reaching an arm out to Amanda's shoulder.

He gently moved Amanda round. Her eyes were gaunt and raw. Wilfred felt his heart beating again, faster than it should have. He tried to think of something to say to Amanda that would make it better, but instead his words left him.

Amanda could hold back her tears no longer. She cried so painfully that it tore through Wilfred. He held her close and let her weep into his shoulder. But no amount of love he could give her would make the pain go away.

Chapter 6

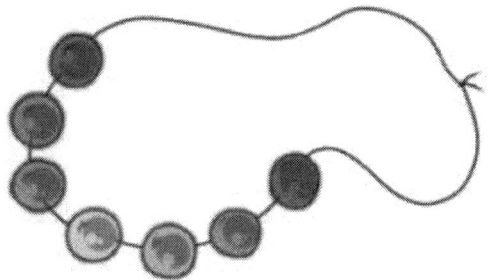

Desperate Times

Ashfeld, Present Day

The sunlight poured in through the windows and broke through the gaps in the curtains. Amanda felt the rays on her and she turned away from them, but in the end, the light proved to be too strong to resist and they broke through her closed eyelids. She rubbed her eyes, slowly opened them and then let out a huge yawn.

Laconically walking to her windows, she opened the curtains and peered out across Ashfeld. It was a lovely day today—the sun was in the blue sky, the birds were singing—it was just the most perfect day that she could imagine. She opened her windows and breathed in the fresh air, filling her lungs with the feeling of accomplishment.

"Perfect day," she said to herself. It was indeed going to be a perfect day for her. Today, she would hand over Daryl to the boy's

Chapter 6

parents, get the reward and pay off all her debts. All her money problems were going to be solved. She could barely contain her excitement.

Amanda went to the next room and knocked on Daryl's door. "Daryl? Daryl, wake up."

Daryl didn't respond. Amanda knocked again. "Daryl? Come on, time to get up. Early bird catches the worm."

Still he didn't respond. *Lazy kid.* Amanda didn't want to waste too much time getting Daryl to his parents, so she opened the door and just went in. "Come on, Daryl. Time to get up." Daryl didn't stir from his bed. Amanda pulled the curtains open to let some light into the room. "Wakey, wakey, we got a long journey ahead of us. We got to get going if we want to meet your parents . . . DARYL?"

Amanda cried in shock when she saw that the bed sheets had been pulled to one side and Daryl wasn't there. "Oh, no, no, no, no . . . Daryl?"

Frantically, she pulled the covers off the bed, thinking that he may be hiding underneath them at the end. He wasn't. She checked under it. He wasn't there. "Come on, Daryl, this isn't funny!"

If she lost Daryl, she lost her chance of getting any kind of reward. Panic set in as she ran down the stairs. "Daryl? Daryl? Where are you kid? Come on, where are you?"

She threw open doors wherever she could—but it wasn't until she charged into the dining room and saw Daryl sitting at the table, did she relax. "Oh, you gave me a fright there!"

"Morning, Amanda," Daryl said, looking up from his work. He pressed a small, pointed piece of charcoal against a sheet of paper, moving it around in circles and zigzags. By his side, Wolvie panted and stood to attention, as if standing guard by the child.

"How about some breakfast?" Amanda asked. "I got some fruit if you want?"

"Okay, then."

The word "please" wouldn't have gone amiss, Amanda thought. Sighing, she grabbed her fruit bowl from her larder and brought it over to the table. As she put it down, Daryl took an apple from it and handed it to Wolvie, who gnawed it down hungrily. Daryl then took a piece of fruit for himself. "What are you doing, Daryl?" Amanda asked.

"Drawing some pictures," Daryl replied. "Like this one?"

Daryl held up his latest creation—a rather scribbled picture that looked like a very thin bat with razor sharp wings. It was very messy and certainly nothing that would appear in any art galleries. But then, Daryl was only a kid.

"What is it?" Amanda asked.

"It's a dragon," Daryl said. "Look, that's its wings, its long neck and its horns and . . ." He pointed to the end, where it looked like a tree was bursting from its mouth. "That's it breathing fire!"

"Cute," Amanda said, feigning interest. "What's that around it? Mountains?"

"Huh?"

"Those scribbles around it, are they supposed to be mountains or something?"

"Oh those? No, they were just on the page before I started drawing."

"Oh, okay . . . wait. Where did you get the paper for that?"

"I found it in that drawer over there." Daryl pointed towards the set of drawers near Amanda's potion mixing table.

"What?" Amanda followed Daryl's pointed finger, noticing that her sets of drawers were open. Panic set in as she looked through the rest of the drawings that Daryl had done. And then horror. "These are my potion mixing scrolls!"

"I couldn't find anything else," Daryl protested. "Hey, can I show you this really neat picture I did?"

Amanda frantically looked through the pieces of paper, hoping that Daryl had left at least one of them intact. But all of them had some scribbled image of some kind on them. The pictures had been drawn over the writing on the scrolls, leaving most of them virtually unreadable. In some cases Daryl had torn them from where he was pressing too hard. "Some of these scrolls are over one hundred years old!" Amanda snarled.

"Hey, do you want to see this picture?" Daryl exclaimed, somewhat oblivious to Amanda's indignant response. He held up a picture that he had drawn earlier. "I drew a picture of you, me and Wolvie—you like it?"

Amanda didn't even look at it. She snatched it from Daryl's hand and took all the bits of paper, shoving them back into her drawer. "If anything is in those drawers, it means *don't* touch!" Amanda shouted.

"Sorry," Daryl apologised, "I just couldn't find any paper."

"Then you *wait* till I'm awake and then you *ask*!" Amanda snapped back. She sniffed the air. "What's that smell?"

Chapter 6

She followed her nose. The smell became stronger the closer she got to her bags of ingredients. It was a stale, putrid smell—and it seemed to be coming from there. She opened one up—and gasped in horror.

"OKAY!" she screamed, turning to Wolvie and Daryl. "Who put that in there?"

Wolvie whined and lowered his head.

"Wolvie really needed to go," Daryl said.

The veins on Amanda's neck started to bulge, her skin went deep red and she looked like she was about to explode from her flesh any second.

"You don't look so good," Daryl said. "Are you ill?"

"Ill?" Amanda grunted, barely able to contain her rage. "Do I *look* ill to you?"

Amanda's eyes turned red, like a monster was about to break forth. When she spoke, her voice sounded at least two octaves deeper—every word she said was like thunder and shook the room. Daryl whimpered and hugged Wolvie.

"You're scaring me," Daryl cried. Wolvie echoed this sentiment with a terrified whine.

"Oh you don't know *anything* about being scared yet, boy!"

There was a knock on the door. Amanda immediately snapped out of her red mist and turned to look, like a frightened cat sensing danger. She turned back to Daryl and Wolvie, who were cowering in fear. "You two stay there," she warned them. "And DON'T. MOVE!"

Amanda shut the dining room door and took deep breaths as she went to answer the door, pinching the sides of her head with her thumb and forefinger. *Damn it, Amanda, you almost lost it again.*

She opened the door. Berger was standing there, arms folded and scowling. "Oh, Miss Berger!"

"I heard noises," she said. "Is everything all right?"

"Oh yeah, yeah, fine . . . ," Amanda said. "Just . . . having an argument with . . . myself . . ."

Berger's expression didn't change, making Amanda even more nervous. "Er . . . I was making a new ingredient for a potion and . . . I didn't agree with it so . . . I . . . had an argument with myself . . ."

Berger sniffed the air. "Is that . . . dog I can smell?"

"Huh? What dog?" Amanda stuttered. "I don't smell any dog . . . can you smell dog? I can't smell anything."

Wolvie's howl came from the dining room, causing Amanda to scowl, embarrassed.

"You're not keeping a pet are you?" Berger asked. "You know I have a strict no-pet policy."

"Er . . . no, it's not a pet, I promise you. It was . . . it was . . ." Amanda then tried to put on her best sad face. "It was a poor wounded animal I found on the side of the road. I'm just trying to nurse it back to health. It'll be gone when it's healed, I swear."

"All right," Berger said. "Amanda, I was thinking about what we talked about yesterday. And I think that I wasn't right in what I said to you."

"Oh," Amanda said. "Well, that's nice of you to say, Miss Berger."

"As in I was being *too nice*," Berger said suddenly. "Therefore, I want my money by the end of today!"

"Today?" Amanda stammered. "You said I had a week!"

"And you told me you would have my rent for me last month," Berger replied back. "You either have the money for me by night time—or you're out!"

"Fine," Amanda sighed. "You'll have your money tonight. I promise."

"How many times have I heard *that* before?"

"No, I swear. Hand on heart, it'll be with you tonight. If not, I'll move out myself!"

"Tonight," Berger said sternly. "No more chances."

Amanda closed the door and let out a huge sigh. "Having an argument with myself," Amanda chastised, slapping the side of her forehead. "What was I thinking? Stupid, STUPID!"

Berger's new demands certainly put a lot more added pressure on her than she needed right now, but they were still doable.

Wrightson isn't too far away if we make a move, Amanda thought. *If I leave now, I'll be there before lunch . . . and assuming I can find Daryl's parents and pick up the reward, I can be back before sundown.*

With a steely resolve, she walked back to the dining room. "Daryl, I'm sorry if I was angry earlier. I didn't mean to— WWAAAGGGHH!!!"

Wolvie had cocked his leg up and was weeing over a few more of her ingredient bags. "No, no, no, no!" Amanda rushed over to try and pull him away, but he was still doing his business and the dog wee went everywhere. When Wolvie had finished, Amanda checked to see if any of the ingredients were salvageable—but Wolvie had marked his territory over most of them and wee had soaked through to the contents inside. Amanda would have to throw them all out— losing much of her stock.

"Bad wolf!" she screamed at Wolvie. "Very bad wolf! You just lost me about a weeks' worth of ingredients!"

Wolvie whined and looked up with puppy dog eyes.

"Don't you give me that look, young man!" Amanda grunted. "Ewww, I got dog wee over my hands."

She washed her hands in a basin whilst Daryl comforted Wolvie. Amanda often wished she had better control over her temper. Drying her hands, she turned back to Daryl, putting on a false smile. "Hey, you know what day it is today?"

"What?" Daryl asked.

"It's the day we find your parents," Amanda exclaimed.

"It is?" Daryl beamed.

"Yes," Amanda replied. "But we have to get moving quickly. So pack your things and let's get going."

"But I don't have any things to pack."

"Great! We can get moving straight away then!"

"Oh, before we go, can we visit Dunaway River?" Daryl asked. "I've heard it's the longest river in the whole country. It could feed the whole of Draconica. And they say just one drop can quench your thirst! And, and... you could wash the whole of Brittana and Celtland combined *and* you'd still have enough left to—"

"LOOK KID! DO YOU WANT TO SEE YOUR PARENTS AGAIN OR NOT?"

Amanda covered her mouth, surprising herself at that outburst. "I'm sorry. It's just that, er... we need to get going soon. The sooner I can get you back, the sooner I can claim my reward."

"Reward?"

"I mean... the sooner I can reunite you with your parents!" *Stupid Amanda! Watch what you say!* "They are probably worried about you, you know. We'd best not keep them waiting."

"Oh right!" Daryl cried. "Hear that, Wolvie? I'm going to see my parents again. Thanks, Amanda, you're the best!" He ran out of the dining room.

"Yeah... don't mention it," Amanda whispered.

Amanda slowly opened the door to her house and looked out. The streets were fairly empty at present, what with it being early morning. Good. She wanted as few people as possible to see her leave with Daryl—just in case someone else had seen the poster and was looking for the reward. "Okay, let's get going."

Amanda had attached some supplies to the end of a stick, wrapped in a cloth. It wasn't much, but it would at least help them along the journey to Wrightson and back. She kept Daryl close to her and Wolvie followed behind. Amanda decided to take the back way out of Ashfeld, to be as discreet as possible.

"How long before we get to see my parents?" Daryl asked.

"We should be there just after lunchtime if we're lucky," Amanda replied. "Just stay close to me, and don't wander off."

Daryl put his hands around her waist.

"What are you doing?" Amanda asked.

"You said stay close to you," Daryl said.

"Not *that* close."

"Oh . . . sorry . . . " Daryl let go.

"HEY YOU!"

Amanda stopped in her tracks and slowly turned round, the lump in her throat digging into her. The giant man from yesterday pounded towards her, rolling up his sleeves.

"Oh hi," she said. "How are you?"

"I've been looking all over for you!" the man shouted at her. "You owe me a refund!"

"Ah, yeah, that," Amanda said. "Look, I was going to come back to you about that." She was about to speak, but then remembered Daryl was nearby. "Um, Daryl, will you give me a few minutes?"

She walked closer to the big man and moved in closer, speaking as quietly as she could so that Daryl couldn't hear. "I'm just about to get myself a huge cash sum . . . when I come back I *swear* that I'll pay you back. Cross my heart, hope to die!"

She went to leave, but the big man put a giant hand on her shoulder. "That can be arranged!"

"Hey, leave my friend alone!" Daryl shouted at the big man.

"Beat it kid," the man shouted back. "Now, listen here, witch! You owe me after the bad potion you sold me—not to mention some compensation for the emotional stress you caused me. If I don't get it soon . . . wait . . . is that a . . . moon wolf?"

Chapter 6

He noticed Wolvie and gasped in amazement. "I didn't think they existed anymore. Tell you what, if you let me have that creature, we'll call it even."

"So, all I have to do is give you this wolf and you'll wipe the refund?" Amanda thought about it. "Deal."

She would be glad to get rid of the creature after all the problems he caused her.

"No!" Daryl cried, holding onto Wolvie. "He's mine! You can't have him!"

"Daryl," Amanda said firmly. "Hand the nice man the wolf." If it was one less thing that she could get out of her hair, Amanda was happy to see the back of the wolf.

"Noooo," Daryl said, looking like he was about to cry.

Seeing his eyes go wet, Amanda felt a little bad and she changed her mind.

"I'm sorry," Amanda said to the big man, "but I can't let you have this wolf."

"You said we had a deal!"

"We didn't shake on it," Amanda said, matter-of-factly.

"Boglins to you!" the man snarled. "You said I could have the wolf and I'm not leaving without it!"

"You stay away from Wolvie!" Daryl shouted back.

"Out of my way, kid!"

The man grabbed Daryl and threw him to one side. Daryl scraped his leg on the ground and he let out a cry of pain. The man turned towards Daryl, seeing the poor lad cry his eyes out and clutch his knee.

"Sorry, kid," the man said, turning to Daryl. "I didn't mean to hurt you. Here, let me have a look at that knee."

He lifted up Daryl's leg so that he could get a better look at the bruise. His eyes raised in surprise when he saw the mark on his leg. "Wait . . . I know that mark."

Amanda gasped and covered her mouth. *No, how stupid of me!*

"That's the mark on the poster," the man said, a smile raising. "If I hand you in . . . then I'll be rich!" He turned to Amanda. "You can keep the wolf. I'm taking this boy!"

"GET AWAY FROM HIM!"

Amanda didn't have time to try and negotiate with the man. She held her hand towards him and then flung it back in the other direction. He was lifted up by an invisible force and thrown many feet back into barrels of fish. Amanda ran towards Daryl and cast a healing spell on his leg to fix the wound. "You all right?"

"Yeah," Daryl replied.

The man burst from the barrel with a roar, now angrier than ever. *Oh, I shouldn't have done that!* Amanda thought.

"No one humiliates me!" he shouted. "I'm going to break your bones!"

"Daryl, can you walk?" Amanda asked.

"Yeah, I think I can," Daryl replied.

"Good. Then run!"

"Run? But why?"

Amanda pulled on Daryl's sleeve, sprinting ahead and pulling the child behind her. Wolvie followed in quick succession as the large man thundered after them.

"Come back here!" he bellowed.

Within a few seconds, he had closed the distance between Amanda and him. She couldn't understand how someone as tall as him could be so fast. Outrunning seemed to be a pointless tactic; so she decided to put her faith in magic. She blasted the ground with a thick layer of frost, creating a frozen sheen of ice. The man slipped and fell on his backside, sliding around. He tried to stand, but could not gain a good footing and so fell down again. By the time he was able to stand, Amanda and Daryl had disappeared.

The man let out an angry growl at seeing his prey get away from him, slamming the ground like a furious gorilla. Then he whimpered and walked away, kissing his damaged knuckles.

Chapter 7

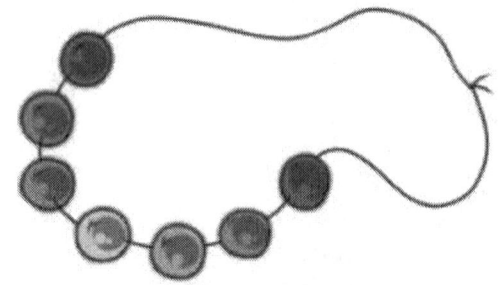

The Journey to Wrightson

Forest of Celt

"**A**manda . . . ," Daryl moaned. "Can we stop for a moment? I'm tired."

Amanda didn't pay much attention to Daryl as he complained, trundling onwards through the forest. She wanted to put as much space between her and the large gorilla that may be following them—and also to cover as much ground as possible. She needed to get to Wrightson as quickly as possible so that she could drop off Daryl and get her reward. That's all she was thinking of right now. It was the only reason why she was even doing this to begin with. The *only* reason.

"Keep up, Daryl, we got a long way to go."

"But I'm tired," Daryl complained, plodding behind. "I didn't get much sleep last night."

"Why not?"

"I couldn't sleep, so I spent the night drawing."

"And whose fault is that? Now come on, we've got a long way to go and we won't get there by moaning."

Daryl let out a huge moan.

"What did I just say?"

Wolvie rubbed up against Daryl as if giving him some support. But Daryl looked like he was about to fall asleep at any moment. Wolvie licked the side of Daryl's face. Daryl jerked awake. "You're a good boy," he said, stroking Wolvie's head.

Amanda looked back. Daryl and Wolvie seemed so happy together. He had really latched on to the wolf. A part of her hoped that his family would allow him to keep the wolf when she returned him to his parents. Somehow, she doubted it though—wolves were generally not kept as pets in the modern world.

Daryl caught up with Amanda, forgetting his fatigue. "Hey, Amanda . . ."

"Yes?"

"Can I ask a question?"

"If I say no will you do it anyway?"

"Those gems around your neck, they give you your magic, right?"

"Yes." *How many more times do I have to tell him this?*

"So, if I wore them—will I have magic powers?"

"It doesn't quite work that way," Amanda replied. "You have to know how to manipulate the energies to control them. Only some people have the ability to control magic."

"Why?"

"I don't really know," Amanda replied. "From what I read, magic in its rawest form is unpredictable and dangerous, and no mortal can control it directly. You need to use magic items to command it, but only some are born with the latent ability to do so."

"So, you were born with the power to control the magic?" Daryl asked.

"Well, magic items anyway," Amanda replied.

"So, that orange one—that gives you fire, right?" Daryl asked, wincing a little at that.

Amanda sighed. She thought she had explained this a hundred times already.

"Yes."

"And green is healing, right?"

Chapter 7

"Yes."

"And blue is ice?"

"No. White is ice. Blue is wind."

"So . . . ," Daryl sniggered. "The blue gem gives you wind?"

"Yes, the blue gem gives me . . . HEY!"

Daryl laughed. Wolvie let out a wolfish snigger also. "You're funny."

"Yeah, whatever," Amanda sighed.

"Amanda, are my parents really at Wrightson?" Daryl asked.

"Oh of course," Amanda replied. "And I'm sure they'll be happy to see you."

"They survived the fire?"

"Fire? What fire?"

"The fire at my village."

Amanda looked somewhat concerned as Daryl told his story.

"My parents told me that they would come after me, but then a fire started. I waited for them, but they never came."

Amanda turned round, eyes widened. "You . . . poor thing . . ."

"Maybe they did get out, but why didn't they wait for me?" Daryl looked towards Amanda hopefully. "You . . . saw them, right?"

"What?"

"You said you spoke to them, that's right isn't it?"

Amanda felt a guilty sensation eating inside her. She knew it was wrong what she was doing, exploiting the poor child like this. "Daryl, I . . ."

But when she saw the hope and desperation in Daryl's eyes, she didn't have the heart to tell him anything other than what she had said. "Of course I did. They told me to make sure that you were okay and to bring you back safely."

She knew it was dishonest what she did, but the lie made Daryl happy. And if he was happy, then she could still claim her reward at the end. *Just keep thinking of the reward.*

"That's great!" Daryl exclaimed. "And when I meet my parents again, I'm going to ask that you come stay with us."

"What?" Amanda gasped.

"You've been so kind to me, I'd hate for you to go back and live on your own."

"Well, that's very sweet, but . . ."

"Nope! I won't hear of it. I'll tell my parents to keep you and we'll all live together. You, me and Wolvie. You could be part of our family."

"Family?" Amanda asked. "Well . . . that would be nice. I guess."

Just keep thinking of the reward.

Just keep thinking of the reward.

Just keep thinking of the family.

Reward. I mean reward.

I mean . . .

Family . . .

"Amanda?" Daryl then asked. "What does that red gem do?"

Amanda put a hand to the gem, as if trying to hide it. "You don't want to know. It's dangerous. One of the most dangerous magic gems there is."

"Well, why do you have it then?"

Amanda chose her answer carefully. "So no one else has to, I guess."

Amanda often wondered herself why she kept such a dangerous item around. But she believed it was better in her hands than of someone who would abuse its power.

Daryl put his hand to his ear, as if hearing a sudden sound. "Hey, I think I hear a river. Maybe it's the Dunaway River! Come on, Amanda, let's have a look!" He ran off in the direction of the sound.

"Daryl, don't wander too far," Amanda said, following him.

Luckily, Daryl didn't wander too far and she quickly caught up with him. Daryl was standing by the side of the river. He stood and looked, gasping in awe. "Wow! It's so pretty."

The river was pure and clear—a crisp looking blue colour. It was the purest looking river that Daryl had ever seen. Many had often said that the Dunaway River had magical properties, making it clearer than other rivers.

"This . . . ," Amanda gasped. "This place feels familiar."

Wolvie let out a couple of howls and barks.

"What is it Wolvie?" Daryl asked.

Wolvie was sniffing a nearby tree.

"Do you need to go again?"

Daryl followed the direction of Wolvie's nose, which was pointing to a carving in the wood. It was a crude looking carving of what looked like a heart—and inside had two names. "Wilfred . . . Amanda . . . Hey, Amanda. Is this you?"

Amanda moved closer to have a look. Her eyes almost popped out of her head. "Oh my gosh . . ." She looked behind her towards the river. "This . . . this is where Wilfred and I had our first kiss."

Amanda walked closer to the river, almost ignoring Daryl and Wolvie. "I haven't been here for years. It was when me and Wilfred first started going out. We were wandering around the forest until it got dark. Then we found this part of the river. The way the moon shone down and lit it up—it was so beautiful. Then Wilfred suggested that we go for a dip. He pretty much pulled me in the river. We splashed around for hours. Then, at the end, when we were laying on the side drying off—we . . . well, maybe I'll tell you when you're older!" She turned back to the tree. "We carved our names here so that this would be our special place forever." Her voice stammered and she croaked a little. "We never came back here again."

Wolvie rubbed his nose against Amanda, whining softly.

"Are you . . . okay?" Daryl asked.

"Yeah," Amanda said, taking a deep breath. "I'm fine! Really, I am . . . Say, how about we stop here for lunch?"

"Yay!" Daryl cried.

The trio set up their place near the tree and sat down to have a modest lunch of fruit, cheese and bread—which were the last few supplies that Amanda had in her house. But Daryl seemed happy enough with the food.

Wolvie munched on a piece of fruit that Daryl fed him. Amanda never thought of wolves eating fruit. She remembered Wilfred also had a thing for fruit as well. She always saw wolves as carnivores. Still, if he was happy then she wasn't complaining. Daryl nibbled on a bit of cheese whilst Amanda took a drink of water.

"So . . . how did you and Wilfred meet?" Daryl noticed that Amanda looked a little down after asking that. "That's . . . if you don't mind me asking."

"No, it's all right," Amanda sighed. "I suppose it doesn't do any harm for you to know. Well, I first met him at least . . . five years ago. Back in my old home of Cantasham . . ."

The Journey to Wrightson

Cantasham, Five Years Ago

Amanda wiped down the bar, cleaning it of any loose traces of alcohol that had been spilled on it. The tavern was quite busy tonight and she was on her own as the owner had snuck out to see his "special mistress." Amanda didn't mind. This was a good place to work and something to help her pay the bills whilst she set up her potion business.

A loud cry came up from the miners' table across the way. These men worked in the local diamond mine and, regular as clockwork, they had come here after work to enjoy their ales. It sounded like they had had a busy day as the amount of ale they had so far was substantial. But they were a respectable lot and never caused any problems for anyone.

Sitting between them, leaning back in his chair, was Wilfred Adamtine—son of Lord Adamtine. His father owned the mine and, by birthright, he didn't need to do any work as everything was catered for him. But he always seemed to enjoy hard labour and worked with the miners. And they respected him for that.

Wilfred turned towards the bar, his bright blue eyes shining towards her. Amanda's heart went aflutter and she lost herself in their brightness. It had been like that the first time she laid eyes on him.

Then she remembered that he was a Lord himself and she shouldn't be looking at him that way. She went back to her duties, making sure the bar was clean for her boss when he got back.

"Look's good to me."

When she looked up again, Wilfred was leaning over the bar, looking at her, smiling. Amanda gasped aloud, but she straightened herself up and coughed loudly.

Chapter 7

"What . . . what can I get you, My Lord?"

Wilfred threw a single coin onto the bar. "For your thoughts," he replied.

Amanda picked up the coin, confused. "Lord Adamtine?"

"Wilfred," he replied. "Call me Wilfred."

Amanda was in shock—a Lord that was allowing a common folk girl to call him by his name? That was unheard of!

"And as for the coin," Wilfred said, "I figured since *you* aren't going to speak to me, I'd figure I'd make the first move."

"Oh," Amanda gasped. "Um, well that's a turn up for the books."

In truth, Amanda *had* wanted to speak to Wilfred—but being that he was of noble standing she knew someone like her wasn't really worthy to talk to him. But now that he had made the first move, she didn't know what to say.

"I guess you're busy looking after the bar," Wilfred said. "What time do you finish work tonight?"

"Oh," Amanda stammered. "Um, I'm here till closing . . ."

"I see," Wilfred said. "Well then I'll have to wait till then." He turned and walked away, but then looked back. "And just so you know, I'm not leaving until I get to speak to you."

He went back to rejoin his comrades. Amanda had to pinch herself to make sure she was still awake. Keeping her cool, she walked round the back of the bar, out of view from anyone. Then she jumped into the air with a "yes!"

After closing time, Amanda brewed some mint leaf tea for her and Wilfred. Wilfred leaned back in his chair as Amanda brought him his drink. Although the tavern did sell tea, it wasn't a very popular drink in this bar (due to the residents preferring some of the harder stuff) and so this was the most action the tea cup had seen in years.

Wilfred picked up the cup and sniffed it, taking in the aroma of the drink. "Smells nice," Wilfred said.

"Hope you like it," Amanda said nervously. "It's my own recipe."

"I'm sure I will," Wilfred said, smiling. He took a sip of it, letting the taste roll around his palette without it burning him. "Mmmmm, I'm detecting a subtle hint of brazen mint in this drink. This is a Valenco recipe, if I'm not very much mistaken?"

"Yeah. You been to Valenco?"

"My father has a villa out there," Wilfred replied, describing it as if it was the most ordinary thing in the world. "I've spent a little time out there myself. But you're not from Valenco."

"How did you guess that?" Amanda asked, surprised at his powers of deduction.

"You have the 'Celtland look,'" Wilfred replied, referring to her brown hair and green eyes.

"Yeah," Amanda replied. "I was born in Celtland. I moved to Valenco when I was about five."

"Really? Why?"

"Er . . . I . . . don't really like talking about it." As much as she fancied Wilfred, she wasn't sure she could trust him with the *whole* truth yet.

"I understand." Wilfred didn't press the subject any further. "So what made you come back here?"

"Well," Amanda continued. "I stayed in Valenco until I did my degree at the university. But, I couldn't really get much work at Valenco, so I decided to move on."

"What did you study?"

"Alchemy. Yeah, I know. The irony—an alchemist not being able to find work in Valenco of all places."

Amanda looked at his blue eyes for more than a second and instantly she forgot how to speak. It was like Wilfred's beautiful blue eyes made her swoon.

"You okay?" Wilfred asked. "You look nervous."

"Oh, sorry," Amanda apologised. "I'm just not used to being talked to by such a handsome man."

"Really?" Wilfred leaned on the table. "You think I'm handsome?"

Amanda realised she had let that slip without trying. "Yes, I mean, no . . . I mean . . . well, you are a little . . . I mean . . ." She became all flustered and went bright red. "Am . . . am I still talking? How about we talk about you for a bit?"

"No," Wilfred replied. "Let's talk about you tonight."

"Really? You want to hear more from me?"

"Of course," Wilfred replied, taking another sip of his tea. "Please continue. What made you come back to Celtland?"

She and Wilfred talked until the early hours of the morning. They both went to work exhausted the next day—but for them, it was worth it.

Chapter 7

And they would meet up after work many more times after that.

Forest of Celt, Present Day

"Did he know you were a sorceress when you went out with him?" Daryl asked.

"Actually, I wasn't back then," Amanda said. "I mean, I always kind of had an interest in magic to begin with—though don't ask me why. I didn't really become a sorceress until . . ." Amanda paused. "Until . . ."

"What happened?"

"Something . . . terrible. I hoped that magic could fix it—it didn't. I kind of, lost control. After that, no one trusted me. But by then I had already learned a little about magic. It seemed a shame to not use what I had learned. I hoped that I could learn to control it, maybe try and master it. It actually helped me out with a few things in life—problem is that a lot of people tend look at you differently if they learn you use magic."

"Why?"

"Magic is looked down upon since the Age of Sorcery ended. In the old days, people used to use magic in everyday life—but it caused too much damage. Now that people have forgotten about that, they rather not give it the time of day."

"So . . . what happened? What made you turn to magic?"

Amanda looked down and closed her eyes. It wasn't a memory she liked to revisit. "I lost a baby."

"Oh," Daryl said. "Did you ever find it?"

"No . . . ," Amanda replied. "I mean I *lost* a baby. As in . . . I never had one. I hoped that magic could help fix me, but in the end it destroyed everything I loved."

"I thought you said you liked magic?"

"That's the irony. I do like magic, in fact I think I enjoy having it. But it took away everything from me. I found out that there were certain gems that could give you magic powers, so I went about collecting them. They actually aren't that hard to find if you know where to look. There was this one gem that I thought could help me."

She held up the Blood gem. "This gem—it's a Blood gem—was supposed to be the answer to all my problems. This gem's magic is supposed to heal the user. I thought it could heal me. But, there were some . . . side effects. Which I found out the hard way. Despite that, I was desperate to learn how to control it. No other gem I had came close to helping me. So I studied hard every waking moment. It became an obsession for me until . . ." Amanda sighed hard. "Until Wilfred walked away from me."

She wrapped her arms around herself and looked away and closed her eyes, feeling some tears starting to build up. Daryl could sense that she was upset and he didn't like that, not when she had been so nice to him. "Well, I'd never leave you if I was your husband."

Amanda laughed. "If you were my husband, I think I'd be hauled off to jail!"

"I didn't mean that," Daryl laughed. "I just mean that I'd never leave you."

"You wouldn't?"

"You're nice."

"You're really sweet, you know that?"

Just keep thinking of the reward, Amanda thought. *Don't get too attached.*

Daryl took another bite out of his cheese. Then he looked towards the Dunaway River. The water looked so crisp and cool. Daryl smiled. "Let's go for a dip," Daryl said. He took his shoes off and rolled up his trouser legs, then ran into the shallow part of the river. He kicked the water to splash it around. "Come in, Amanda, it's warm."

"Maybe another time," Amanda said.

"Aww, spoilsport."

He took a huge handful of water and threw it towards Amanda, splashing her from face to belly. Amanda wiped the water from her face and looked at Daryl in disbelief. He looked worried, wondering if he had angered her again.

Then, she smiled. "Oh . . . you are *so* dead!"

She ran into the river, grabbing handfuls of water and throwing them at him. Daryl and Amanda laughed as they splashed each other. Amanda couldn't remember the last time she had laughed like this—at least not since she and Wilfred were here. She had often joked with Wilfred that, when she had a child of her own, she would do this with them.

"Come on then!" Amanda laughed. "Give me your best shot!"

Daryl picked up as much water as he could and threw it at Amanda, getting her all wet and soaking her gown.

Chapter 7

"Oh, that's your best shot?" Amanda laughed. "Have a taste of this!"

She summoned up a large amount of magical energy, directing it to the water around her. The water spun round her and she forced it towards Daryl—but in her excitement she used too much. A massive tidal wave shot forth, crashing into Daryl.

"Ha!" Amanda chuckled, breathing on her knuckles and then rubbing her gems. "Never get into a fight with a sorceress. That's important lesson number one, Daryl. Daryl?"

She noticed that Daryl wasn't there. Gasping, she frantically looked around but couldn't see him.

"Daryl? Daryl?"

She looked down the river, where she noticed in the distance that the tidal wave she created was travelling down. Her eyebrows raised in terror.

"No," she gasped, suddenly realising that Daryl was in the part of that tidal wave when she cast it. "Daryl! Hang on, I'm coming!"

Chapter 8

Torn Between Duty and Love

Castle Gryphenpyre, Wrightson

Luthar's footsteps were slow as he walked through the courtyard, stopping by a statue. He drew his sword and knelt down, holding the handle and placing the blade on the ground.

The statue was of a beautiful woman, kneeling down and holding a bunch of flowers. An inscription on the pedestal read QUEEN SHEENA GRYPHENPYRE. 16 OE–11 NE. It originally said LOVED BY ALL, but this had been defaced and was barely readable. The statue looked every bit as beautiful as Sheena when she was alive. The artist had done a painstaking job capturing her beauty to the last detail.

It was one of Luthar's best works—and one that he had been proud to sculpt.

Chapter 8

As he looked at the statue, he fought to hold back his tears. Shame ate away at his heart.

"I'm sorry, Sheena . . ."

Luthar had been a great war hero who had come into great acclaim for his actions during The Gothon Campaign—where he defended a village singlehandedly. Because of that, Queen Sheena had asked him if he would like to join the Royal Guard, an honour that only a few were granted.

Sheena had only been granted the title of Queen Regent around that time—her father, the King, had taken ill and Sheena had been appointed to rule in his place. It was the first time that Luthar had ever seen her. How radiant she looked that day—her beautiful golden hair seemed to glisten as she gave him her Royal Blessing.

Previously, war had been the thing he had enjoyed the most. Until he met the Queen. Over time, she became his best friend—and so much more. When her father died and she became Queen, he was there for her. He was her confidant. There was never a happier time in Luthar's life than when he was with Sheena.

And Kimera took that away from him.

His mind flashed back to that dark forest and the biting cold rain that fell from the sky, numbing him to the bone. He, Sheena and Kimera were returning from their journey to Brittana, having visited the Queen of Brittana (of whom Sheena was friends with), whom recently had had her own child. She and Sheena spent the time swapping tips with each other. It was a happy occasion for all involved.

But on the way back, they were set about by bandits, dressed in black hoods. They chased Luthar, Sheena and Kimera to the edge of a cliff, cutting off their escape. And even in the dark, Sheena could see it was a very long drop to the bottom. One wrong move and they would fall.

Luthar fought the bandits off as best as he could, keeping them away from Sheena. He remembered he fought with fire that night—every strike made against the bandits was with as much fury as he could gather. The very idea that they would try and harm the Queen was abhorrent to him and he would see to it that they would not go unpunished.

A stray bolt hit Sheena in the shoulder, knocking her off her horse. Kimera was there to help his sister before she could tumble. He stayed around her, keeping her protected. Daryl's cries thundered across the air as Sheena kept her baby close to her. Even an injury would not part her from her child.

Luthar saw this and tried to help Sheena, but Kimera shouted back, "I'll keep my sister safe, you just keep the bandits back."

Luthar nodded, swinging his sword at another bandit. His blade carved through the cloth of the bandit's cloak and it fell from him, making Luthar think that he had decapitated him at first. The bandit struggled to grab his cloak again—but it was too late. Luthar had already seen the silver and green armour that lay underneath—the sigil of the Gryphenpyre family.

Luthar realised that these were not bandits—they were Royal Guard.

This shock made Luthar lower his guard and the "bandits" were on him. They wrestled his weapon from his hands and dived on him, locking his arms behind his back and forcing him to the ground. But Luthar was a strong man and he overpowered them the first time, until more guards jumped on him. They punched him in the stomach and across the face to weaken him, whilst others restrained him and forced him to his knees.

Sheena looked on in horror as Luthar was restrained. She had also noticed that the bandits were her own Royal Guard. "Stop this at once!" Sheena called out. "Your Queen demands it!"

The Royal Guard didn't stop and Luthar was beaten until he spat blood. "Stop it!" Sheena cried. "Kimera, help him!"

Chapter 8

She saw Kimera standing over her with a sardonic smirk. His finger rubbed across Sheena's crown, feeling its texture, admiring its beauty. "You know, it must be such a burden to carry a heavy object such as that on your head. Such a . . . heavy . . . burden . . ."

He lifted the crown off her head as his sister stared, dumbstruck. Luthar looked on, his eyes widening in terror as Kimera slowly lowered the crown over his own head, savouring every single second until he just dropped the crown down. Thunder crashed as the golden headgear landed on top of him and Kimera spread his arms out, laughing manically.

"Well, what do you know—it fits."

Sheena's eyes were filled with horror and disbelief. She clung tightly to Daryl as he cried into her shoulder. Kimera gripped Sheena by the shoulders and lifted her up to her feet, planting her near the cliff. Luthar struggled against the guards, but they kept him where he was. He was unable to do anything. Kimera held his sister's shoulders and looked into her eyes, still smirking. His sister's heartbroken expression filled him with more joy with each passing second.

"You know, I've never seen you apart from that boy since he was born. Your dedication to your child is quite extraordinary."

Sheena felt a biting pain in her stomach.

"I do hope that you and Daryl will keep each other company—on your journey to the Afterworld."

Kimera pushed on Sheena's shoulders and she found only air to stand on.

Luthar screamed as Sheena vanished over the edge of the cliff, the screams of Daryl echoing through the air, drowned out by the roaring thunder. His agonised scream was lost in the thunder and he lowered his head down, his tears mixing in with the rain.

When he raised his head again, he saw Kimera looking at him, the hideous smirk seemingly forever tattooed on his face. In his hand he held a dagger, caked in the blood of his sister. Seeing her blood enraged Luthar and he tried to get to his feet, summoning all his strength to break free. But the guards continued to hold him down.

"Easy there, Captain," Kimera sneered.

"I am *not* your Captain!" Luthar shouted.

"Oh really?" Kimera gasped. "But you are dressed as a Royal Guard. Have you forgotten the oath you swore on your inception? You serve the Crown and the interests of your Monarch. And—last time I checked, I believe your monarch was...who was it now? Oh yes . . . *me*. You serve me now, Luthar."

"I will *never* serve you!" Luthar grunted through gnashed teeth. "I'll die before I give my life for you."

"What of the life of your mother?"

Luthar gasped.

"You honestly think that I wouldn't have planned this to the very last detail? Your mother is being watched closely. If you even think of doing anything stupid . . . well, I don't think I need to tell you how much she will suffer before she dies. So . . . what's it going to be . . . Captain?"

Luthar wished he could have done the right thing that night. He wished he could have just broken free and pushed Kimera over the side of the cliff then fight his way back to his mother. He wished he could have done that.

But instead, he bent his knee and offered his service to the new King. Something he hated himself for.

The blackmail that Kimera held over him still existed to this day. And Kimera always made a point to let Luthar know what would happen if he betrayed him.

It was this—not honour—that made Luthar Kimera's slave.

He had tried a few times to get his mother out of danger, but Kimera seemed to be one step ahead of him. He made this threat very seriously and Luthar quickly found out that nothing he did would be able to save her. He had no choice but to obey.

Sheena would have been horrified to see what he had become.

"Captain."

The voice broke Luthar's train of thought. He found himself back in the courtyard, a shadow looming over him. He looked over his shoulder.

"Here again are you?" Kimera sneered.

"I'm mourning your sister," Luthar growled.

"Ah, yes, I see," Kimera said, indifferent to Luthar's pain. "Well, I'll allow you a moment to grieve. Okay, moment's over. Now I believe you have to find the child."

Luthar tried to hide his snarl as he got to his feet. "Yes, Your Majesty."

"Good." Kimera walked away from Luthar. "Don't waste your time mourning my sister. She isn't worth any tears."

Chapter 8

Luthar felt his hands tighten around the handle of his blade. It was just him and Kimera alone in the courtyard. One strike would end it all. Luthar didn't even stop to think about the consequences. He crept up behind Kimera.

"My sister really cared for you, you know."

Luthar stopped in his tracks, lowering his sword. Kimera turned round, his sneer seemingly etched on his face. "You honestly didn't think I knew about your little affair? I saw the way you looked at each other. My sister thought the sun shone out of your backside. And yet," he moved closer, "in the end you couldn't do *anything* to protect her."

Luthar could feel the rage boil inside him, but he suppressed it deep down inside.

"You must really hate me," Kimera continued. "But just remember what happens if anything should happen to me. That really must hurt you most of all." Kimera looked back at the statue, grimacing. "You know, I should have that statue destroyed. It's such an eye sore." Then he walked away.

Luthar turned back to the statue of Queen Sheena, wondering what she must be thinking of him from the Afterworld. Sighing, he walked away.

Chapter 9

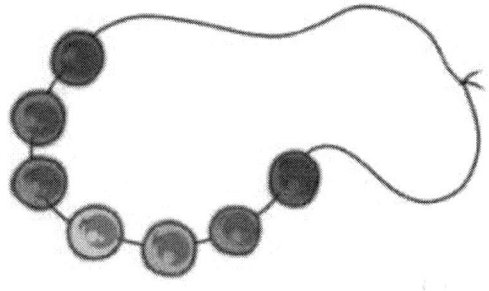

Rescue of Daryl

Dunaway River

Amanda charged across the stream as fast as her legs could carry her. Wolvie ran across the side of the river, his nose to the ground to try and catch Daryl's scent. "Wolvie. Can you sense him?"

Wolvie looked back, panicking.

How could I have been so stupid? I lost control again!

Sometimes Amanda forgot how powerful the magic she controlled was and that led to dangerous things. In her excitement, she used too much power for the water spell and ended up blasting Daryl away. She couldn't believe she had done something so terrible.

I hope Daryl is okay.

Wolvie suddenly picked up the pace, letting out loud barks.

Chapter 9

"What is it, Wolvie?" She struggled to keep up with the wolf as he ran ahead of her.

Please be okay, Daryl.

Wolvie stopped at the end of a waterfall and looked over, howling.

"What is it? Can you see him?"

Wolvie pointed his nose downwards. Amanda followed his gaze. The bottom of the waterfall led to a somewhat secluded part of the river with several, sharp rocks lined around the bottom. For a horrid moment, Amanda thought that Daryl would be splattered across the rocks—dead because of her mistake. But following Wolvie's nose, Amanda breathed a sigh of relief when she saw Daryl was still alive.

He was hanging onto a loose tree branch by the waterfall, having clung onto it. Daryl was trying to pull himself up, but the branch was damp and he was slipping.

"DARYL!" Amanda cried.

Daryl didn't hear her; he was too busy trying to maintain his grip on the branch. Thankfully it looked like it was a sturdy branch that could support Daryl's weight—but she was sure that he couldn't hang on forever.

"Hold on!" she cried out. She reached towards him, focusing all her psychokinetic energy. She hoped that she could just grab Daryl and lift him out—but this magic had a limited range and required Amanda to be fairly close to objects in order to move them. "Come on, come on!"

Daryl was too far away. Amanda cursed to herself. "Stay there! I'm coming for you!"

If only she could use psychokinesis on herself, she could have just hovered down and grabbed Daryl. Unfortunately, her powers didn't work that way. She would have to do this the hard way.

Amanda sat down by the ledge and then gently eased herself down the side, grabbing onto anything she could that would support her—be it a root, a rock or something else. The side of the cliff was damp and somewhat slippery, and Amanda's hands and cloak became caked with mud.

Her hand slipped whilst trying to grab a rock. Were it not for the strong root that she was grabbing onto, she would have fallen. She caught a look down. Whilst not a long drop, a fall like this would certainly break some bones. But to Daryl, being smaller and not as physically strong as Amanda, it could do a lot more.

She could feel her limbs start to tremble as she lowered herself down, taking her time as much as she could. Amanda was not used to this much physical exercise—usually the hardest thing she had to do was pull out a stopper from one of her bottles. She usually let her magic take care of the rest. Now she was starting to sweat from all the effort. *If I survive this, I'm getting some more exercise*, she told herself.

Amanda took several more moments to climb down and reach Daryl. One of his arms fell from the branch and he flailed around madly, trying to regain his grip. Amanda picked up her pace as much as she could to try and get to him in time.

"Daryl!" she called out. "Hang on!"

"Amanda!" Daryl cried. "I'm slipping!"

"Hang on, I'm nearly there!"

Amanda found the strongest thing she could hold onto by the wall, and with her other hand, reached out to him.

"Take my hand!"

"I can't," Daryl shouted back. "I'm scared I might fall!"

"You won't! You trust me, right?"

Daryl smiled and looked back at her. His face relaxed and his eyes glowed with hope. He reached out. "I trust you!"

Now that he was in range, Amanda could use her magic to lift him closer. Daryl floated up slowly.

Beneath them, the water started to bubble and churn, a hideous shape rising from it.

"Hang on, just a little further," Amanda gasped. The strain of having to concentrate on Daryl whilst holding onto her own weight was exhausting. But Amanda persisted, gritting her teeth. And then she felt Daryl's soaking palms in her hand.

"I got you!" she cried. "Okay, let's get you out of—"

Wolvie started snarling above them. "Wolvie?" Amanda asked, looking up. "What is—"

A tentacle wrapped around Daryl, causing him to scream in terror. He looked down. "What . . . what is that thing?"

In the river below was an abomination of a creature. Its head looked somewhat like a giant toad, but with writhing tentacles as limbs. It appeared to be made of the very water that surrounded it—leading Amanda to just one conclusion. Her eyes widened in horror. "It's a . . . ghul . . ."

Ghuls were supernatural monsters, made from the very elements themselves. They could be summoned through the use of powerful spells—but that was often not advisable, given that ghuls were mindless beasts. So what a ghul was doing here, Amanda did not know.

"Pull me up!" Daryl cried. "Pull me up!"

Amanda pulled Daryl as hard as she could, but the ghul countered this by pulling on Daryl. He was ripped from the branch and Amanda was dragged along with him. They crashed into the river, but luckily they didn't break anything on the way down. The ghul tugged on Daryl with its tentacle, trying to bring him into its open jaw.

"Hang on!" Amanda cried. She tried to grab the tentacle, but her hands went straight through it. The ghul's magical energies kept it together, and each time Amanda tried to grab it, it turned to water again. There was no way that she could keep a hold of it. She summoned up her ice magic.

"Get off my boy, you freak!"

She blasted the tentacle with a cold blizzard, freezing it solid. The ghul cried aloud in what sounded like pain, even though ghuls were supposed to be incapable of feeling any kind of emotion or feeling. Using all her strength, Amanda smashed the ice around Daryl. She rushed towards Daryl, her feet soaked with each step. She took Daryl in her arms to warm him up; he shook from both the cold of Amanda's attack and the fright of the monster.

"You okay?"

Daryl wrapped his arms tighter around Amanda. "I'm okay."

"Let's get out of here."

But before they could, two more tentacles shot towards Daryl and Amanda, wrapping themselves around their waists. From up high, Wolvie howled and roared.

Amanda held up her hands to blast the creature again, but this time another tentacle wrapped around her wrists, forcing her hands together tightly. The ghul applied pressure around them until Amanda could barely feel her hands. Most of her magic had to be expelled through her palms in order to be cast, but now that they were tied up, she couldn't do a thing. Amanda and Daryl were pulled towards the water ghul's mouth slowly, where rows of sharp teeth awaited them.

Wolvie could take no more. He dived down the ledge without any care for his own safety. His incredible agility helped him get down without any problems. Wolvie charged towards the tentacles holding his friends and ran through them with lighting fast speed. Amanda and Daryl fell in the water just as Wolvie turned to the ghul.

"Yeah! Go get him, Wolvie!" Daryl cried, getting back to his feet.

Wolvie arched his back and bared his teeth. The ghul unleashed many tentacles towards him, but Wolvie was too fast. The wolf ducked and dodged, running into the ghul and ripping it apart slightly with his razor sharp teeth. The ghul was just too slow for Wolvie and it looked like the courageous moon wolf would easily win.

Unfortunately, during a leaping attack, another tentacle grabbed Wolvie in mid-air, finally having the poor wolf at its mercy. It threw Wolvie into its mouth.

"No! Wolvie!" Daryl cried.

They could still see Wolvie inside the water ghul, struggling to get out. The creature was trying to drown him from within. Wolvie struggled, but could not break free. And the poor wolf could only hold his breath for so long.

"Don't worry," Amanda said to Daryl, her right hand turning ice cold. "I'll get Wolvie out of there."

She summoned up an enormous blast of ice magic and sent it towards the ghul. The creature was instantly frozen on the spot, turning into a giant iceberg. Hoping that she held back her magic enough to keep Wolvie intact, she blasted fire towards the ghul. The heat, mixed with the intense cold, caused the ghul to shatter and melt.

She rushed towards Wolvie to make sure that he was still in one piece. The wolf coughed and spluttered, getting rid of the water in his lungs. "You okay, boy?" Amanda asked.

Wolvie looked up, let out a little whine and rubbed his nose against the side of her face. Amanda stroked his head. Whilst she found him annoying at first, she was starting to like him now.

"Wolvie!" Daryl cried. He ran and put his arms around the wolf in a hug. Wolvie whined happily.

But the happiness had to be put on hold once Amanda noticed that the water was reforming.

"Oh, give me a break!"

It seemed that nothing Amanda could do would stop the ghul. Behind her, she saw that Daryl was cowering in fear near Wolvie.

Amanda knew that she had to stop this ghul—leaving it to roam freely would be too dangerous.

But there was also another reason that she wanted to destroy this ghul. Something that she never expected to feel.

He tried to hurt Daryl.

Seeing Daryl scared brought up a rage inside Amanda—like her maternal instincts had burst forth. Daryl may not have been her child—but she would defend him to her last breath!

That gave her an idea.

Having now seen how easily it could reform, Amanda now knew that as long as the ghul was near water, it could regenerate. She had to separate it from the water.

And she had one power that could help her.

Not all her magic required her to use her hands to summon— there was *one* particular magic that she could expel a different way. This was not really a spell that Amanda used very often, because of the potential of destruction—but it was the only spell that could destroy the beast.

"Daryl, you and Wolvie keep back," she warned the child.

"What are you going to do?" Daryl quivered.

Amanda looked back at the creature. "Let's just say—I'm about to blow this ghul away."

Channelling her magical energy through her lungs, Amanda inhaled a deep breath. The air pressure around her picked up and the water seemed to be dragged towards her. She took in an incredible amount of air—more than any human could. By the time that the ghul had completely reformed, Amanda had filled her lungs. She pursed her lips together and her cheeks puffed up as she started to blow. As the air left her mouth, it spun round like a tornado, picking the ghul up from the ground. The air pressure in the centre of the tornado evaporated all moisture and water, causing the ghul to disappear. Cut off from its main element, the ghul could not reform and, with a watery cry, it was swallowed up by the roaring wind and vanished into oblivion.

Amanda took a few seconds to regain her breath. She forgot how much this magic left her out of breath if she used too much.

"Wow!" Daryl gasped. "Amanda, that was amazing!"

"It was nothing," Amanda said, trying to sound nonchalant.

"Are you okay?"

"It's . . . pretty exhausting," Amanda replied, slumped over. She caught her breath. "Daryl, I'm so sorry that happened. It's my fault.

Chapter 9

I sometimes lose control of my magic and . . . well I guess I went over the top there . . ."

"It's all right, I had fun!"

"Fun? You nearly died!"

"But you saved me, so I didn't."

"Yeah . . . ," Amanda said. She then did a double take. "Yeah, I did . . ."

Daryl smiled at her. Amanda smiled back, somewhat nervously. "Hey, come on, let's climb out of here."

When they had left, the man in black emerged from his hiding place, stroking his chin thoughtfully.

Impressive, he thought. *Amanda is growing stronger. I wonder if she even realises her true potential?*

He opened the pages of his book, landing on the page with a picture of Amanda and the ghul. The picture perfectly captured how Amanda destroyed the ghul—right down to the very last detail.

The climb going back up to the top of the ledge was surprisingly a little easier than climbing down. Lifting her arms over the edge, she grabbed some grass and pulled up, happy to be landing on soft ground once more. She lay down on the grass, catching her breath. She felt Wolvie's tongue against her skin. "Hey, easy, boy!" Amanda laughed, trying to stand up. Wolvie jumped on her, as if giving her a hug. "Oh, well you're very welcome."

She did a sudden double take, seeing that Daryl and Wolvie had reached the top before her, even though she thought they were behind her. "How did you . . . get up here so quickly?"

"I walked up the path."

"What path?"

"That path," Daryl said, pointing to a path that led downwards. It was something that Amanda had missed in her haste. "Wolvie found it."

"Of course there's a path," Amanda sighed. She looked at her dress, which was so caked in mud it was practically a different colour. "Oh, this is my favourite gown. I better wash it. Can't go to Wrightson looking like a tramp." She looked towards Wolvie and Daryl. "Er, boys . . . Why don't you give me some privacy for a little bit?"

"Okay," Daryl said. He stood where he was.

"Maybe you should . . . go hide in a tree for a bit. I need to . . . wash my dress. As in . . . take my dress off . . ."

"Oh, I see," Daryl said. "Okay, we'll give you privacy." Daryl turned and walked away with Wolvie, but then stopped and turned back. "Amanda?"

"Yeah?"

"Am I really your boy?"

"Sorry?"

"You told that ghul I was your boy."

Amanda looked back, surprised. "Did I?"

"Yes, you did. Am I . . . your boy?"

"Um . . ." Amanda thought quickly. "Sure . . . yeah, you're my boy. Best boy . . . haha."

"Good," Daryl said. "Then you're my best girl!"

"Awww, how sweet. Now, er . . . if you don't mind . . ."

"Oh sure, of course." Daryl and Wolvie disappeared into the bushes to let Amanda do what she needed to do.

Did I really say that? Amanda thought.

Don't get too attached. You have to hand the boy over to get your reward.

Amanda looked back, seeing that Daryl wasn't there. *Right. Right.*

Chapter 10

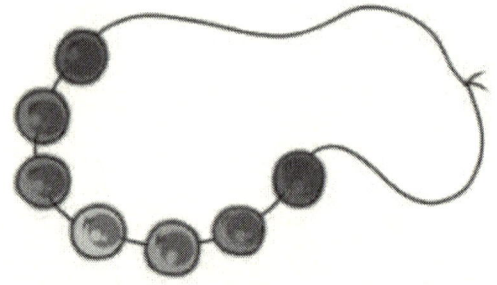

Handing Over the Reward

Wrightson

The rest of the journey was fairly uneventful. They arrived at Wrightson two hours later—a little later than Amanda had hoped, but still within the time frame to get the money back in time if they did this right.

They stepped out of the forest and into an open area overlooking the city of Wrightson—the capital of Celtland. It was a beautiful city, the buildings made from the most beautiful white stone Celtland could offer. It stretched for miles across with beautiful white battlements protecting it. The castle itself was at the very top of the city, overlooking everything below. The banners of Kimera flew in the breeze all around the perimeter—way more than there needed to be. It was almost as if the King wanted everyone to know where they were—as if they could ever forget it.

Handing Over the Reward

It was only about a half an hour walk away, if that. Amanda was so close that she could almost taste that gold.

Though a part of her would be sorry to see Daryl go.

"Well," she stammered. "Here we are."

"That city is huge!" Daryl exclaimed.

"Well, that's the capital for you," Amanda said. "Always has to be the biggest. Well, shall we get going?"

Daryl turned to Amanda, almost looking tearful.

"What's wrong?" Amanda asked. "Aren't you pleased that we're going to be finding your parents again soon?"

"Yeah, I am . . . ," Daryl said. "But I'm sad for you."

"Really?"

"I can't bear the thought of you all alone. You're too nice a person, you need someone to look after you," Daryl said. "Why don't you stay with us?"

"Oh . . . er, well . . . That's nice, but—I got, things at home to take care of . . ."

"Like what?"

"Like . . ." Amanda struggled for an answer. "Like . . . my potion business. Yes, I need to focus on that."

"You can move here and do it," Daryl suggested. "You said that people don't like you up there anyway, maybe you can do it here instead? You could ask my parents, I mean they know you, right?"

Daryl really didn't want to take no for an answer. And Amanda didn't want to let on that the reason she was being so negative was that she didn't want to tell Daryl that she had been lying to him about meeting his parents. But then again, the poster did say that his family was waiting to be reunited with him, so they had to be alive. But Amanda wasn't sure if she was ready to interact with the outside world just yet.

"Look, Daryl . . . er . . . maybe we should just get you to your parents and then maybe we'll talk about it, okay?"

"Okay!" Daryl looked really excited. "Hear that, Wolvie? We're going to meet my parents again. I'm going to ask if we can keep you too!" He rubbed Wolvie's ears and made the animal pant happily. "Come on, Amanda, let's get going!"

Daryl rushed past her with Wolvie.

"Sure . . . let's get going . . ."

Amanda kept telling herself that she was only doing this for the reward. Nothing else. All she had to do was hand the boy over to his parents and that was it. Her task was done. Nothing else mattered. Her bills would be paid up and everything would be fine.

Except . . .

She had come to like Daryl. In the short time he had been with her, she had formed a connection with him—something she couldn't explain, but felt strong about it. It was a connection that she had never felt with another human being in a long time.

I called him my boy.

She shook her head and slapped the side of her face. "Get a grip on yourself!" Amanda snapped at herself. "You want to live on the streets all your life? Just think of the reward! That's all that matters."

"Amanda?" Daryl called back, "Are you okay?"

"Er, yeah I'm fine!" Amanda called back. "Coming!"

Amanda followed after him. Her heart felt heavy with each step.

There were two burly looking guards at the entrance to the city dressed in silver and green armour. One of them had a scar across his face and the other had a big, bushy beard that was in desperate need of a trim. As Amanda stepped forward, the guards closed their pikes together. "Who goes there?" the bearded guard cried.

"And a good morning to you too, gentlemen," Amanda said back, politely.

"State your business," the scar-faced guard asked in a gruff voice.

"Er, I'm here to . . . er . . ." Amanda found herself very nervous around these big, scary guards. Considering she had gone up against a ghul, she thought she'd be a little bit braver. "I'm bringing this child back to his parents . . . Marcus and Glenda. They live here."

"Never 'eard of them," Beardy pouted.

"Do you know *everyone* in the city?" Amanda asked.

"Only the important ones," Beardy replied.

"No one's allowed to enter, unless you pay a toll," Scarface said.

"A toll?" Amanda protested. "But I'm returning this boy to—"

"I don't care," Scarface snapped. "Everyone that enters the city has to pay a toll, by order of His Majesty, King Kimera Gryphenpyre. Rules are rules."

"Fine," Amanda groaned. "How much?"

"Fifty Celtland gold."

"FIFTY?" Amanda exclaimed. "What is this, a city or a private club?"

"No gold, no entry."

Handing Over the Reward

"Er, guys look . . . ," Amanda whispered in their ears. "I'm a little short on cash at the moment. But I've been promised a *big* reward if I return this kid to his parents. Why don't you let me through and I'll pay you back when I leave?"

"A reward you say?" Scarface and Beardy looked at each other and both gave a knowing smile. "Okay—but you got to give us something in return."

"Like what?" Amanda asked.

"Your dress," Beardy said.

"What?" Amanda gasped. "I'm not giving you my dress!"

"No dress, no entry," Beardy insisted.

"Yeah, now come on, get it off, love."

Scarface reached for Amanda, taking her by the arm.

"Hey, get your filthy hands off me!" Amanda pushed him away.

Scarface didn't take kindly to that—he was used to women doing what he asked. He pointed his pike towards Amanda's throat. "I should skewer you for that!"

"What is going on here?" Luthar ran towards the two guards, furious. "Have you forgotten your manners?"

Scarface and Beardy went back to their original poses.

Luthar bowed before Amanda politely. "My apologies."

"It's okay," Amanda said. "No harm done."

"Even so, that is no excuse for my men to behave like animals," Luthar said. "How can I be of assistance?"

Amanda gestured towards Daryl, still hiding behind Wolvie. "I've come to return this boy to his parents," she said. "I was told that they would be here."

Luthar gazed towards Daryl. His eyes widened in surprise—the boy had beautiful golden locks and bright eyes just like . . . Queen Sheena. He could never in a million years forget the Queen's beautiful golden hair and this boy seemed exactly like her.

Could it be?

He had to be sure. "Does he have a birthmark on his leg?"

Amanda nodded.

"Can I see it?"

Amanda felt sure that this man didn't mean them any harm—and even if he did, she would break his bones if he tried to harm Daryl. Amanda turned back to Daryl. "Daryl, I need to show this man your birthmark."

Chapter 10

"Okay," Daryl said, a little suspiciously. He lifted up his trouser leg to show Luthar. Luthar got a good look at the birthmark. Exactly how he remembered it. He gasped in surprise—this woman had brought back Daryl, safe and sound.

"I . . . I saw you fall . . ."

Daryl looked back at Luthar, confused. Luthar shook his head, trying to be professional. His moment of joy was replaced with a sense of horror when he realised that he had to return Daryl to Kimera. How he hated duty sometimes.

"You did the right thing bringing him back," Luthar said, even though he actually didn't believe that himself. "Follow me."

The guards stepped aside as Luthar turned to enter the city. Amanda started to follow, but turned back when she noticed that Daryl was still hiding behind Wolvie. "Come on, Daryl," she said in a gentle voice, holding out her hand to him. "We'll be reuniting you with your parents very soon."

Daryl took Amanda's hand. She smiled at him and Daryl smiled back. With Wolvie following behind, they both entered the city.

They walked through the city of Wrightson, passing through the back streets and through the city centre. Luthar walked ahead of them, not speaking.

Amanda noticed that there were Kimeran guards posted at various positions throughout the city—maybe a few too many of them. Even in a capital city, it seemed a bit excessive for this many guards to be around. Amanda saw that the people of the city kept their heads down and seemed to mind their own business—almost as if they were afraid to even speak. Amanda heard a shout to her left and turned round to see some guards attacking a peasant for reasons she didn't know. One of the guards pulled a sword.

Amanda took Daryl by the side of his head and moved him closer to her. She was getting a bad feeling from this place already. His parents couldn't be here in a place this dangerous, surely? If they were, she hoped that they would leave as soon as Amanda reunited them with their child.

"So," Amanda asked Luthar. "Where do Daryl's parents live?"

"Just keep close," Luthar replied, a little gruff. "We'll be there soon."

He led Amanda and Daryl towards the castle.

Handing Over the Reward

Castle Gryphenpyre

Kimera groaned pleasurably as the warm water wrapped around his body. The bath was a large hole in the marble floor, at least 15 feet across. It was enough to fit at least twenty people in—and in the past it had. But Kimera liked to keep this one for himself and refused to share it with anyone. The bath steamed as he lay back and sighed. He could feel the water getting a little bit cold at one part—and he liked his bath a specific way.

"More hot water!" Kimera ordered, clicking his fingers. Instantly, a servant appeared with a jug of boiling water, pouring it into the bath to keep the temperature hot. However, as he poured it into the water, some hot water splashed onto the King. "OW! Are you trying to burn me?"

"M-my apologies, Your Majesty!" the servant stammered.

"You did that on purpose!" Kimera shouted, pointing at the servant. "Assassin! He's trying to burn me! Guards!"

Despite the servant's protesting, he was pulled away by guards, who hauled him off to the dungeons. Luthar entered the bath house, kneeling before King Kimera. "My King, apologies for disturbing your bath."

"This had better be important, Luthar," Kimera snapped. "My bath is very important for relaxation."

"My King," Luthar said, looking up. "The boy has been brought to us."

Kimera was so excited when he heard the news that he barely even dried himself. His royal robes clung to him somewhat and his hair was dripping wet as he thundered into the throne room with a few bodyguards. Upon seeing Daryl, Kimera ran towards him, a beaming smile spreading across the entirety of his face. "Is it you? Is it really you, Daryl?"

Luthar sighed hard. "He has the mark, Your Majesty. It's him!"

Kimera turned to Daryl, his smile large and somewhat creepy looking. Daryl clutched the back of Amanda's dress. "Daryl, no need to fear me."

"Er, Your Majesty," Amanda said, doing a light but nervous curtsy. "I . . . have the boy . . . I brought him back . . . er, me . . ."

"Oh yes, very good, you have our thanks," Kimera said. "Run along now."

"Er . . ." Amanda tread carefully with what she said next, knowing that Kimera was easy to upset. "I . . . seem to remember a reward somewhere? Maybe?"

"Reward? What are you talking about, woman?"

"We *did* offer a reward for Daryl's return, Your Majesty," Luthar reminded him.

"Oh yes, so we did," Kimera pouted. "That's the problem with putting things on paper—it makes it so much harder to take them back afterwards." He clicked his fingers to some guards. "Get this woman her reward, will you?" The guards ran off.

"Reward?" Daryl asked. "What reward?"

"Aha," Amanda giggled nervously. "Don't worry, Daryl. Just something I was promised for bringing you back. So, Your Majesty, when will Daryl be with his parents again?"

"Parents?" Kimera asked. "What are you talking about?"

"The poster said that his family wants to be reunited with him."

"*I'm* his family," Kimera snarled.

"You . . . are?" Daryl asked.

"You don't remember me?" Kimera asked. "I'm your Uncle Kimera."

Amanda's eyes raised in surprise. "Uncle Kimera?" she looked back at Daryl. "Then . . . that means that Daryl's . . . a Prince?"

"Yes, yes, yes . . . We'll easily rectify that," Kimera told her.

"What about my parents?" Daryl asked.

"What parents?"

"Glenda and Marcus."

"Glenda . . . and Marcus?" Kimera thought for a moment and then smiled heartily. "Oh, those two. Yes. I remember them now. We burned them with the rest of the village."

"What?" Amanda asked.

"They were one of the first people to burn," Kimera chortled. "It was actually quite amusing." He then spoke in a high-pitched voice and flailed his arms around madly. "'Oh! Help! I'm on fire! Oh, this really hurts! I'm going to be sore tomorrow! Argh! Argh! I'm burning!'"

Daryl and Amanda stared blankly at Kimera's callous joke. He simply smirked back, locking his hands together. "Too graphic?"

Daryl turned to Amanda, confused. "You told me my parents were okay. You said you spoke to them."

Amanda felt her stomach churn and her throat clog up.

"You mean you *lied* to the boy just so you could get him here?" Kimera gasped. "That's deceitful, despicable, deplorable! I like it!"

"You . . . lied to me?" Daryl asked, his eyes starting to glisten with tears.

"Daryl," Amanda stammered. Now that her lies were out in the open, she found it really hard to try and explain herself. "Look . . ."

"You told me I could trust you."

Daryl's horrified expression broke Amanda's heart and she found it hard to look him in the eye. "I . . . I had money problems," she tried to explain. "I needed to pay off some bills. I . . . look I swear I never meant to lie to you, it was just . . . the only way I could get you to come."

"You only brought me here to collect a reward?"

"No, I mean . . . well yes . . . but . . . I really enjoyed being with you."

"Yes, this is all very nice, but can we move this along?" Kimera sneered. "Daryl is *my* family. So if you don't mind . . ."

Wolvie stepped in front of Daryl, snarling towards the King.

"Ewww, what a horrid mutt."

"Sire, that is a moon wolf," Luthar gasped. "They are sacred animals . . ."

"Whatever, just get it out of my sight."

Two guards took Wolvie by his fur and pulled him away from Daryl. Wolvie snarled, but the guards fought to restrain him.

"Wolvie!" Daryl cried.

"Young man, you're coming with me!"

Kimera grabbed Daryl by the arm and pulled hard against him.

"Let me go, you're hurting me!" Daryl tried to pry himself from Kimera's grip. When that didn't work, he bit into Kimera's palm.

The King yelped and released Daryl. "You little . . ."

Daryl ran behind Amanda, as if trying to hide. "Amanda! Please protect me."

Amanda looked back at Daryl as he stood quivering behind her. She then looked back at Kimera, his eyes flaring.

"Stand aside and let me have my nephew," he said through partially closed teeth.

Amanda was rooted to the spot in confusion. Her gaze shifted between Daryl and Kimera. As much as she now hated the idea of leaving Daryl with Kimera, he was the King! And even she knew better than to go against the King.

Chapter 10

"Daryl," Amanda said. "Look . . . maybe it won't be as bad. And he is your uncle after all. He has a right to have you . . ."

"Please don't let him take me."

Daryl clung tighter to Amanda's dress, tears rolling down the side of his face. She clenched her teeth and pulled her collar from her neck a little farther away. Confusion took over and she looked back at Kimera again.

"Your Majesty, maybe there's some way we can talk about this."

"I said stand aside!"

Not willing to repeat himself again, Kimera grabbed Amanda's shoulder and pushed her to one side as forcibly as he could. She went down hard; Kimera held nothing back in his strength. His shadow smothered Daryl and he reached towards him with tingling fingers.

As Amanda hit the ground, Wolvie's eyes widened in what looked like shock. He turned his head towards Kimera and snarled, lowering his head as if entering an attack position. With a snarl, he seemed to find extra strength from within, causing him to burst from his captors and leap at the King. He dug his teeth into Kimera's left arm. Kimera flailed around violently to shake off the beast and only managed to do it after several attempts. Several Kimeran guards jumped on Wolvie to restrain him.

Wolvie roared and flailed to break free, biting and scratching at their armour. But his teeth could not penetrate the tough exterior.

"Hold that beast down!"

Kimera looked at his arm as the blood flowed forth. It was somewhat superficial and not as bad as it looked. But even so, he was not prepared to let this insult go unpunished.

"Captain!" he scowled at Luthar, pulling up his sleeve. "Put that wolf to the sword!"

"No, not Wolvie!" Daryl gasped.

"But . . . that's a moon wolf," Luthar protested.

"I don't care if it's a blasted unicorn—do as your King commands."

"But, Sire . . ."

"DO AS I COMMAND!"

Luthar struggled with his conscience again—but he was between a rock and a hard place. He knew that it would be no benefit for him to resist. He drew his sword.

Handing Over the Reward

"Wait," Kimera said. "You're right. I can't ask a man of honour to kill a sacred beast in cold blood." He held out his hand. "Give me your sword."

"Sire?"

"Your sword."

Luthar didn't know why he didn't just cut Kimera down where he stood now and end this. But as much as he wanted to do that, he knew that it would do no good whilst the guards were loyal to the King. He handed over his weapon.

"Thank you." He took the blade in both hands. "It's been a while since I held one of these things." The guards struggled to hold down Wolvie, who was fighting with everything he had. "Keep that beast still."

"No, what are you doing?" Daryl tried to rush to Wolvie, but Amanda held him back. "No, please. Stop him!"

Kimera walked slowly as Wolvie desperately scratched and tore at the guards, unable to break their armour.

"Amanda, please, stop him!" Daryl begged.

Amanda held Daryl back, even though this hurt her to do so. She didn't want this to happen any more than Daryl did. But what could she do? He was the King—even Amanda wouldn't dare harm him.

"Don't look, Daryl," she said, trying to pull him away from what was happening. "Just look away . . ."

Just keep thinking of the reward.

"Amanda!"

Just keep thinking of the reward.

"Please help Wolvie!"

"Look," Amanda cried. "Daryl, just keep thinking of the reward!"

Amanda gasped when she realised she had said out loud what she meant to say in her head.

"I mean, just look away . . ."

Daryl looked up at her, his mouth lowered in shock.

"This is what you get for hurting the King, beast," Kimera sneered at Wolvie.

He lifted up the sword and Daryl looked back, despite Amanda's best efforts to make him look away.

"No, no, no, NNNOOOOO!"

Kimera brought the blade down.

Wolvie let out a painful whimper.

And then he stopped moving.

Kimera handed the sword back to Luthar, not even wiping the blade clean. "Thank you for lending me your weapon, Captain."

Luthar took the blade back and was about to clean it when Kimera held out a hand. "No. Keep the blood on it. I think it will serve as a good reminder for yourself—knowing that it was *your* blade that slew the animal."

Gritting his teeth, Luthar sheathed the blade in anger, disgusted at the lack of respect that Kimera had shown.

Daryl finally broke from Amanda's grip and ran to Wolvie. He ran his hands across his soft fur. Wolvie's eye moved towards Daryl, his breathing slowly decreasing. Daryl's eyes were wet with tears.

Wolvie let out one final breath and his eyes closed.

Amanda was frozen where she stood, unsure of what to say or do. She took a couple of steps toward Daryl.

"You didn't stop him." Daryl turned to Amanda. The look of despair and betrayal in his eyes tore Amanda's soul and she froze. "You could have used your magic to stop him."

"I . . ."

"You really did just bring me here for the reward. Didn't you?"

"Daryl, I'm . . ." She reached to touch Daryl, but he ran from her and into the waiting arms of two Kimerian guards. "Daryl, wait. Please. I didn't intend for this to happen. Daryl, you trust me, right?"

Daryl turned to her, his eyes burning with tears and his lips formed into a malicious scowl. "I hope you enjoy your reward," he snarled. "You deserve to be alone."

Handing Over the Reward

Daryl made no attempt to fight against the guards as they took him by the shoulders, leading him away. All Amanda could do was watch. Daryl's words cut into her heart deeper than any sword ever could. She tried to call out, but in the end her words wouldn't leave her throat. She gazed at the floor, ashamed. When she plucked up the courage to look again, Daryl was gone.

"I thank you for bringing my nephew to me, my dear," Kimera said. "You've saved me a lot of time and effort by bringing him to me."

Amanda gazed ahead, ignoring Kimera's voice. He clicked his fingers in front of her face repeatedly. "Hello? Your King is talking to you."

Amanda turned to him and, without even realising she had said it, told him, "You didn't need to do that."

"I beg your pardon?"

"You didn't need to kill Wolvie." Then, remembering her place, she added on a "Your Majesty" at the end.

Kimera's lip raised to a scowl, his moustache flaring. It was only when he heard the sound of clinking coins that he let his temper settle. "It appears your reward is here."

The two guards returned on cue, huffing and puffing as they carried a huge treasure chest between them. They almost dropped it to the floor, glad to be rid of the weight, and opened it up. It was full to bursting with gold coins, all of them sparkling and almost illuminating Amanda. "250,000 coins, as promised," Kimera said. "You can keep the treasure chest, but I can't spare a cart so you'll have to get it back yourself."

Amanda walked towards the gold and reached in. Her fingers moved across the top, moving through the coins—more coins than she had ever seen in all her life. 250,000 of them. Each of them real and sparkling.

Just think of the reward she had been telling herself this entire journey—and now she had it. All the money she could ever wish for. Enough to pay for her rent, her food, her ingredients. Everything.

And yet, when she looked at the coins, all she could see was Daryl's disappointed face. His look of betrayal reflected back to her 250,000 times.

As valuable as this money was, to Amanda it felt despicable. It chilled her blood just to touch it.

Chapter 10

All this time she thought about nothing but money—now she had it and she could not have been more disgusted with herself.

She slammed the chest shut. "Keep your money."

"What's this?" Kimera asked, surprised. "A bounty hunter that doesn't collect her bounty?"

"I'm not a bounty hunter," Amanda said sternly, looking at the King with narrowed eyes.

"Daryl said something about you not using your magic, you're not a witch are you?" Kimera asked. "Because we burn those kinds of women."

"I'm a sorceress," Amanda replied. "And I didn't use my magic because . . ." She couldn't think of a way of finishing the statement.

"Wait . . ." Kimera clicked his fingers and pointed at her. "You're not that sorceress that went berserk in Ashfeld, are you?" Amanda never answered, but Kimera had already clocked her. "My, my. Luthar, it would appear we have a celebrity in our midst."

"It would appear so, Your Majesty," Luthar grunted.

"So *you're* the infamous sorceress of Ashfeld. The one that lost her child and went crazy, nearly destroying all of the town," Kimera sneered. "Yes, we heard about you. I heard that your boyfriend left you as well. How tragic."

Amanda was too angry to reply. She swallowed hard, trying to tamp down her anger.

"You know, we were going to have you executed for what you did—but you have friends in high places. Very high places actually. Well, I can't stay and chat. I have things to be getting on with. Now, as I'm sure you're aware, we have an embargo on this city—but you did me a favour, so you have my permission to leave Wrightson. And anyway—I doubt my people would want someone as dangerous as you around."

Amanda bit her tongue.

"I'll show her out, Your Majesty."

"Very well. Oh, and Luthar . . ." Kimera pointed to Wolvie. "Clear away that corpse will you?"

Kimera and his retinue turned around and left Amanda. She turned round to the body of Wolvie. Luthar went to pick him up, but Amanda held a hand out. "I got this."

She picked Wolvie up and placed him over her shoulder. He felt remarkably light, despite being bigger than the average wolf.

Handing Over the Reward

"For what it's worth, I'm truly sorry," Luthar said as he led Amanda out.

"You're not the only one," Amanda replied.

Chapter 11

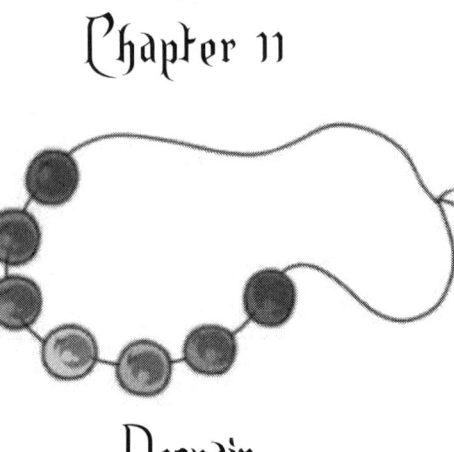

Despair

Forest of Celt

Amanda carried Wolvie's body as far as the Forest of Celt, just as it became dark, returning Wolvie to the place where she and Wilfred first kissed by the Dunaway River. She didn't know why—it just felt appropriate. Amanda placed him next to the tree and sat down in silence for a long time.

"I never meant for this to happen," Amanda said to Wolvie. "All I wanted was to get my reward, reunite Daryl with his parents and that was it. I never thought it would come to this. If I had thought that Daryl's parents were . . . I don't know. Wilfred would be so ashamed of me."

She looked at Wolvie. "You know, it's strange—but you kind of remind me of him. The way you went to fight Kimera. Wilfred did that one time. It was when I was working at the bar . . . a guy gave

Despair

me grief and knocked me over. Wilfred rushed to my defence and really beat the guy up, even though he was several sizes larger than him. I guess . . . that was the first time I really noticed him. I don't know why I'm telling that to you."

She stroked his fur gently, but the wolf had been long dead by now. Amanda leant over and kissed him on the forehead, a single tear falling from her eyes onto his fur. "I'm sorry, Wolvie."

She knew that it would be better to bury him—but just being here was too painful for her. Amanda left Wolvie, hoping that his body would be left alone.

As she walked away, the moonlight shone from above, illuminating the forest area. The river seemed to sparkle with life as the moon lit everything up. Wolvie's fur sparkled, his wound starting to close up.

Ashfeld

Amanda's heart was heavy as she returned home. Her house had never felt so empty before now—or so quiet. As she walked in, she couldn't help but remember when Daryl and Wolvie were around. As annoying as those two were, they did at least bring some excitement into her life. If only for a day.

Sighing hard, Amanda decided to mix some potions—hoping that would take her mind off it. She set up her table, prepared some empty beakers and glasses, then went to check her ingredient bags in the next room. Amanda had to throw out a few of them that Wolvie had fouled, so what she had was somewhat limited. Taking what was left, she then opened up her scroll drawer to see what she could make.

Opening up the drawers, she took out a bunch of scrolls—only to remember that these were the ones that Daryl had drawn on earlier (and ruined). She looked through the pictures that Daryl had drawn. Many of them were very crudely drawn and barely represented what they were supposed to be. One seemed to be a dragon, another a cat, the other . . . she didn't know what. Amanda remembered being angry with Daryl at first when she saw them, but now they brought a smile to her face.

The final scroll (which Daryl had been so keen to show her earlier) had a picture of three characters. Two humanoid, with one of them larger than the other, and the other seemed like a dog. The large person was holding hands with the smaller person. Near the drawings were names and an arrow pointing to each character. An arrow matched WOLVIE with the dog, the other labelled the smaller character as ME, which she guessed meant Daryl. The final arrow pointed towards the bigger character with MY NEW BEST FRIEND.

Amanda closed her eyes, feeling like her soul was being crushed from the inside. She dropped the picture, covered her mouth and fought to keep her tears back. She breathed deeply, hoping to suppress the terrible despair that ate away at her inside.

The door to the spare room was still open—the room that she dared not go in. She walked in slowly, walking towards the cot. This was supposed to be for their newborn child—a child that she lost. Wilfred had designed this cot with her, spending as much time as he could making it. He put all his heart and soul into it. And it was never used. She ran her fingers across it. Her fingers became thick with dust. She looked up at the picture of her and Wilfred, seeing how happy she and him were back then.

She closed her eyes as she remembered the last day she saw him.

One Year Ago

Amanda frantically ripped through the pages of the new book she had, barely stopping to read what was on it. Next to her, several other books lay on her desk, each of them frantically searched through. Amanda's eyes were red and raw, having not slept for days. Her once beautiful brown hair was showing signs of grey. She hadn't eaten in days and was wasting away. But still she persisted, reading through the book at a frantic rate.

She knew that the Blood gem was the key to helping her. It had to be. The stories said it could heal those that used it. She just had to learn to control it. She knew she could do it. She cast the book aside in irritation when she didn't find what she was looking for, then looked through her bookcase for another book. One of these had to have the answers she needed. It *had* to.

She looked up from her book briefly and saw Wilfred standing near the table and eyes raised like he had been caught red-handed. He turned to look at her. The grey streaks had ruined her once perfect brown hair, aging her significantly. Looking at her, you would never have guessed that five months ago she celebrated her twentieth birthday.

"Hello, Amanda," he said nervously.

"Hello, Wilfred," Amanda said. She looked at him for the slightest of seconds and went back to her bookcase to pull out another book. "Maybe this one will . . ."

Wilfred let out a nervous sigh. "Amanda, you need to rest," Wilfred said, somewhat matter-of-fact. "You've not slept or eaten for days."

"I'll sleep when I find the answer," Amanda replied. "It has to be here somewhere."

"Maybe it isn't."

"No, it is here somewhere!" Amanda held up the Blood gem around her neck. "The answer is here! You read the stories—those that used these gems were granted superhuman strength and . . . and the power to *heal* themselves. This can heal me! I know it can."

"It also drove them insane," Wilfred reminded her, forlorn. "Amanda, you know what happened when you tried to use that magic."

"I lost control," she agreed. "But . . . but it's okay, no one got hurt! I know I can control this. I know I can! Then . . . we can be a family. A complete family."

"Amanda. It wasn't your fault, what happened to our child."

"Yes, it was. I lost our baby. But . . . but I can fix it."

"What if it was my fault?" Wilfred suggested. "It was my seed that made you pregnant. Maybe I'm to blame for what happened."

"No . . . no, no, no, don't you say that!" Amanda screeched, running up to him and placing her hands over his face. "You're perfect! You always have been! I'm the one that's defective! I lost our child, I have to fix this. You're not to blame, you're . . ." She then noticed that Wilfred had a backpack by his side and in his hands was an envelope. "You're . . . packed? Where are we going?"

Wilfred took Amanda's hands off the side of his face and lowered them. He looked Amanda in the eyes, even though it hurt him to do so. Holding her hands, he said to her, "Amanda . . . I love you. I always will. But . . . I can't see you destroy yourself like this. This . . . obsession with magic. It's ruining you. And I . . ." He hated having to say these words. "I can't do this anymore."

He handed her the envelope. "What . . . what's this?" Amanda stammered.

"It's a little keepsake," Wilfred replied. "I'm hoping it helps you through the days ahead in some way." Wilfred put the backpack over

Chapter 11

his shoulder. "I've left you some money to keep you going. Goodbye, Amanda."

He turned for the door and walked out of Amanda's life. Amanda felt as if she had been turned to ice. She looked at the envelope in her hands, feeling her blood boil over. She threw it to the ground without even opening it and then charged after Wilfred.

"Fine!" she screamed down the street as Wilfred walked away. "You want to leave, get out of my life—and don't come back!"

"DON'T COME BACK!"

She watched as he walked away. He didn't even turn back.

"Don't . . . ," she whispered, her eyes wet with tears. ". . . come back . . ."

Present Day

A knock at the door pulled Amanda out of her reverie. She went to answer it. It was Miss Berger—and the big guy from the other day.

Not now.

"Hello, Amanda."

Amanda moved away from the door, letting Berger waddle in. Behind her, the big man (who was too big to fit through the door) stayed outside. "Well, the time is now. Where is my rent?"

"And where is my refund?"

Amanda couldn't even look at either of them. "I don't have it."

"What?" Miss Berger screeched.

"What?" the man roared.

"I said I don't have it." Amanda tried to hold her temper, even though a part of her knew that this was not going to end well.

Berger was flabbergasted, her face turned red with rage. "You told me that you would have the rent for me by this time tonight!"

"And where is my refund?" the man shouted. "I want my money back."

"That's it Amanda!" Berger shouted. "I've had enough of you and your lies! If you're not going to pay your rent then I have no use for you."

"I don't care . . ."

"What?"

"I don't care about you . . . or . . . your stupid . . . RENT!"

Amanda flung her arms at Berger, sending a psychic blast that threw her against the man. Both of them were thrown onto the street and crashed into a wall. Amanda walked outside, hands by her side and her eyes narrowed into a vicious stare.

This attracted the attention of a lot of the people in town, who came out to see what all the noise was about. The man quickly got to his feet whilst Berger flailed around on the floor. "Hey! No one makes a fool out of me . . ." He suddenly stopped as a strong pressure gripped him around his neck.

"Why don't you leave me ALONE?"

Amanda's voice turned into a roar, her eyes becoming a deep red—red like the colour of the man's face. He went to his knees, struggling to breathe.

"All you care about is your stupid money," Amanda roared. "What about *my* needs? Didn't you ever stop to think about me? Don't you see how much I've suffered? AREN'T I ENTITLED TO A BREAK?

"Maybe I'll give *you* a break—your neck maybe?"

With that, she turned round to the frightened townspeople, who cowered at Amanda's power. The man was choking now and his skin was beginning to turn a bright purple. But Amanda had no more remorse—she had exhausted all of that. She looked towards the townsfolk, their fear making her feel empowered in a way that she never felt before.

Why should I hold back? she thought. *I've been holding back all this time—and I just feel like letting go!*

It was only when she saw the look of a frightened little boy— which echoed Daryl's disappointed look—that the anger left her eyes.

The man doubled over, coughing madly, lucky to be alive. Everyone stared at Amanda, horror and accusation in their eyes. Amanda held her hands to her head, shocked at her own actions. "Everyone . . . I'm sorry . . . I . . . I didn't mean to . . ."

"It's just like the old days!" one of the townsfolk cried out.

"She lost it again!"

All at once, the townsfolk started throwing verbal assaults and accusations, cursing her for what she did before just a year ago.

Miss Berger was helped to her feet by some townspeople, but she pushed them away. She was so angry with Amanda that she looked like she was about to have a heart attack. "That's it! You're out of here! Gone! We don't want you here anymore! You leave by sunset or we'll throw you out!"

Chapter 11

The people of the town threw similar statements at Amanda. She backed away and then ran into her house, slamming the door behind her.

Amanda looked at her hands. They trembled. She realised that she almost lost it again—just like last time.

She turned to the shelves of books that she had. Each of them represented a quest for her to find the answers to her problem. But what had it gotten her? In the end, she had nothing to show for it but a broken heart, no home, and an unquenchable loneliness.

Amanda screamed and reached for her husband's old woodcutting axe, swinging it to the shelf. Wood and paper flew as Amanda destroyed it and all the contents. She then turned her axe on the shelf of potions, smashing the glasses and spilling their contents. She moved to the work table, turning it into splinters in a matter of seconds. Finally, she charged back into what would have been the baby room, the axe obliterating everything it touched—until only the cot was left. Amanda roared as she lifted the weapon above it.

But then she stopped herself. Gazing at the cot, she remembered that this was supposed to be for her child. The child that she would have done anything to protect. The child that she would have loved with all her heart. The child that she lost.

This cot was built by loving hands, which Amanda remembered used to embrace her during those dark times. Hands that would never embrace her again.

This cot was the only memory she had left—the memory of the last time she was happy.

The axe felt heavy in her grip. She let it drop and fell to her knees, unleashing the tears that she had been bottling up for so long. All her anger, loathing and frustration burst forth in a tsunami of tears. She cried knowing that it was because of *her* that she was no longer

happy, that she was the cause of everything bad in her life.
She cried in that room all night. Alone.

Chapter 12

Tying Up Loose Ends

Gryphenpyre Castle, Wrightson

The cell door opened. Daryl looked up, unable to move from the chair that he was chained to. Kimera walked in with a sneer. "I was worried that I'd never see you again," Kimera said to Daryl. His voice carried no sense of concern.

Daryl said nothing. He looked down, too sad to even cry anymore.

"What, no words for your uncle? I thought you would have had some questions for me."

"Actually, I do," Daryl whispered, looking up. "Why did you burn my parents?"

"Your parents?" Kimera exclaimed. "They never were your *real* parents. As to why I burned them—well, they had to be made an example of."

"But why?" Daryl asked. "What did they ever do?"

"They betrayed their King," Kimera replied. "They kept you from me for six whole years. You, who were supposed to have died with your mother—your *real* mother. You're the only thing that's a threat to my line as King."

"Queen Sheena . . . was my real mother?" Daryl felt more tears coming on. "Why did you kill her?"

"My boy. You have to see it from my side of the story. She was Queen, my sweet, sweet, sister . . . but she didn't deserve to be."

"Why?"

"Why? Because she was too much of a goody-goody." Kimera felt all the venom in his words spill out with each breath. "Father always lavished more attention on her than me, even though I was the strong one in our family. I fought in the military, I was there at the front lines in many wars—but that was never enough for my father. I did everything I could to win that old man's approval—but it was never enough! But my sister, all she had to do was bat her eyelashes and she could get anything she wanted. She never deserved the throne—she was too . . . too . . . ."

"Kind," Daryl replied. "I used to read up on Queen Sheena back in the village. I never knew why, but I was attracted to her story. I guess I know now. They say she was one of the kindest people to ever have lived."

"You don't rule kingdoms by being kind!" Kimera snapped. "Only the most ruthless of those deserve to be King. Look at Emperor Gothon of Baalaria—he had the whole of Draconica in his palms at one point, and he didn't get that by being kind. No, he was ruthless—as I have been. I have proven myself to be the most ruthless King to ever have lived, feared across the land—and rightfully so. This is all I've ever worked for and *no one* will take it away from me! Not you, not my sister, not ANYONE!"

"What are you going to do to me?" Daryl asked.

Kimera smirked. "Why, my boy, I'm going to reunite you with your parents. The same way I did back at the village. There will be a special event tomorrow and you will be the guest of honour. In fact, you're going to go down in a blaze of glory, so to speak!

"Enjoy your last few hours alive. If it's any consolation, at least you'll die warm." He turned to leave.

"You must be very lonely," Daryl said suddenly.

"What are you talking about?" Kimera gawped.

"Being feared by everyone must make you a very lonely person. You wouldn't be that way if you were kind."

Kimera looked away, shaking his fingers quickly. Saying nothing else, he left the dungeon.

The jailers shut the door behind the King as he walked out, still shaking his fingers. "Captain," he said to Luthar, who was waiting outside with two other guards. "Prepare the stake. I want it ready to go by midday tomorrow."

"What for?" Luthar asked.

"Oh, you know, I thought the kingdom could have a nice little barbecue," Kimera replied sarcastically. "Why do you think?"

"But those are only for burnings," Luthar said. "We've not had a burning for over a century."

"We've never had anyone to burn before," Kimera sneered.

Luthar gasped, knowing only *too well* what he meant. "There's no need to kill him."

"Did you think I wanted to find Daryl to *protect* him?" Kimera snarled.

"He's just a child!" Luthar shouted.

"Oh wait, hang on," Kimera said, patting himself down and looking through his pockets. "Oh where is it? I'm sure I saw it here somewhere. Nope. I'm sorry—I can't find a care to give. Now if you don't mind, I believe you have orders to do."

This was a step that Luthar was not prepared to go. "No!"

"I'm sorry?" Kimera asked. "Did I hear you say *no*?"

"I will have no part in this!" Luthar roared. "I have too many lives on my conscience; I won't have a child's life on there too."

"You will have as many lives on your conscience as I *tell* you to have!" Kimera snapped. "Now fall in line!"

"To hell with you!" Luthar shouted. He turned and walked away.

"Don't you turn your back on me!" Kimera shouted. "You get back here now."

"You think I care about what happens to me? I've spent too long having to live with this pain. I no longer care what you do to me."

Luthar continued walking, half expecting a knife to be planted into his back sometime soon. What actually came was more painful.

"What about your mother?" Kimera hissed.

Luthar stopped and turned back.

"Do you care what happens to her? What am I saying? Of course you do. How old is she now? 60? 70? She's getting on a bit. It would be a shame if she was found dead whilst she slept—with a knife in her back."

Luthar charged towards Kimera, but Kimera's bodyguards placed their pikes across to stop him from coming forward. "You go anywhere near my mother and I'll kill you!"

"I don't think you understand, Luthar," Kimera growled. "I am *King*. If you defy me, then the people you love will suffer. Your mother? She will suffer the most for your betrayal. I will put her through all kinds of torture and force you to watch. But I'll keep her alive and make sure that she feels every single moment of pain and suffering. Only *after* I've run out of ways to torture her—then I might do her the mercy of killing her.

"So, what's it going to be, Captain? Are you going to fall in line— or are you going to walk away?"

Luthar felt the rage inside him disappear. With a tear in his eye, he said, "I'll do as you say . . ."

"You'll do as I say . . . what?"

"Your . . . Majesty . . ."

Kimera smiled. "Good boy. Your mother raised a very well behaved lad."

Chapter 13

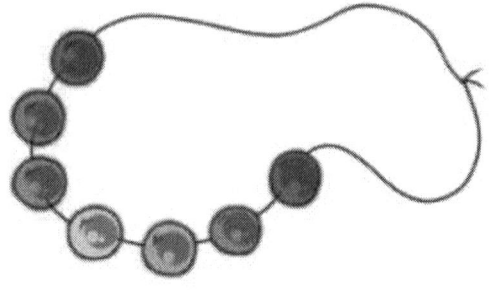

Redemption

Ashfeld

A pounding sound roused Amanda from her broken slumber. She would have loved nothing more than to ignore the sound, but it came fast and loud, threatening to knock the whole house down.

Amanda lifted herself up with a grunt, her bones stiff and her neck aching. She had fallen asleep on the floorboards in the spare room after hours of crying. She moved her neck around, trying to ease it back into shape. Dust covered the side of her face and she wiped it off. The smallest rays of light shone through the window as the sun hadn't even fully risen yet.

The pounding on the front door became more frantic and angry, like the person on the other end was trying to knock the door down. It even sounded like they were scratching against the door.

Seriously? Amanda thought. *This early?*

She knew that the people of Ashfeld wanted her gone, but this early in the day? The pounding increased. "Go away," Amanda shouted. But the pounding on the door didn't stop. "I said go away!"

Still the pounding and scratching continued.

"Can't you just leave me alone for a few minutes?"

The pounding became even more frantic. Amanda could take no more. "All right! I'm going, okay?" She stood up and stormed towards the door, feeling like she wanted to give the person on the other end a piece of her mind. "I get it, you want me gone! I'm going! I won't even bother to pack, I'll just get out! You happy now?"

She flung the door open—and was knocked to the ground as something jumped on her.

"Wolvie!" Amanda gasped.

Wolvie licked Amanda's face happily as if he hadn't seen her in years. "Hey, easy boy!" Amanda chuckled. When Wolvie settled down, Amanda's astonishment began to settle in. "You're alive," she gasped. More than that, the wound he suffered at the hands of Kimera was completely gone—like it was never there in the first place. "How is this possible?"

Wolvie pulled on Amanda's dress, almost like he was trying to drag her out the door. "Wolvie? What are you doing?"

The wolf persisted. Amanda gently pushed him away for fear that he might tear her dress off. "Wolvie, what's gotten into you?"

Wolvie panted nervously, looking around for a way to try and help Amanda understand what he was trying to tell her. He noticed that, amongst the destruction that Amanda had left, there was the picture that Daryl had made of them lying around. He picked it up and handed it to Amanda.

She took the picture from Wolvie, looking at it. Seeing this picture made her heart sad to see it, but when Wolvie moved his nose over Daryl's picture, she understood.

"Daryl?" Amanda asked. "You . . . want me to go to him?"

Wolvie nodded. Amanda sighed. "He won't want to see me," she said sadly. "Besides, he's a Prince. He'll have it all. A big castle. People to look after him. A King for an uncle . . . Wait." A thought just occurred to her. "If Daryl was the son of the Queen, then . . . that means he'll be next in line to the throne. So, Kimera's Kingship will pass to Daryl. Why would he . . ."

Chapter 13

Then she remembered something that Kimera told her.

We'll easily rectify that.

"Oh my gosh . . . ," Amanda gasped. "He's going to kill Daryl!"

Wolvie nodded, grunting. "Wolvie, we have to go to get . . ." Amanda charged towards the door, but stopped before she could get outside, as if she had second thoughts. "What am I doing?" she cried.

She walked back in, found a chair to sit on and placed herself on it, forlorn. Wolvie walked to her, whining slightly. "I'm no hero," Amanda said. "Everything I touch falls apart. I couldn't stop Wilfred leaving me, I couldn't control my anger. I couldn't even . . . I couldn't even look after a baby. How am I supposed to just walk into Wrightson and rescue Daryl? He hates me anyway. He'd probably rather just die."

Amanda's self-loathing and despair brought up a bad feeling in Wolvie. He walked towards the spare room. "Where are you going?" Amanda asked.

She followed the wolf. Wolvie was riffling through the devastation that Amanda had left the night before. He was searching through the debris of the smashed drawers, their contents spilt out across the floor.

"What are you doing?" Amanda asked.

Amongst the mess was old clothing and unused baby clothes. Amanda didn't understand what was going on, and she was a little nervous that Wolvie was rifling through her personal things. "Wolvie, I think it's best that you leave . . ."

Wolvie lifted his head up, holding something in his mouth. He walked over to Amanda and dropped the envelope that Wilfred had given her when he left—still unopened.

"How . . . how did you know this was here?"

Amanda had hidden this away when Wilfred left—and in truth she had forgotten all about it. Now that she had it back in her hands, she remembered being so angry with Wilfred that she just threw this envelope in the drawer and never intended to open it. But now Wolvie seemed to want her to open it. Amanda felt her fingers rub against the smooth paper, moving to the edge of the flap to open it. But then she stopped herself, as if suddenly hit by a deep fear.

Wolvie whined, like he could sense Amanda's fear. He took the letter from her, dropped it to the ground and used his teeth to carefully rip across the top of the envelope.

Redemption

"Wolvie, what are you . . ."

Wolvie took the envelope back in his mouth and lifted it to her. Something fell from the envelope and hit the floor with a light thud. Amanda looked down and gasped as she saw something sparkling.

She picked up the object and held it in her palms. It was a ring, made from the purest diamonds Amanda had ever seen. The ring sparkled like a clump of stars in the darkness. It mesmerised her and, for a moment, it reminded her of Wilfred's eyes.

Amanda looked back at Wolvie, who still had the envelope in his mouth. Taking it from him and wiping off some of the spit, she looked inside, seeing a small piece of paper. Removing it and opening the letter up, she saw that it had been written by Wilfred— she would recognise that clear, precise handwriting anywhere. She scanned the letter in detail, almost as if she could hear Wilfred's voice inside of hers.

My dearest Amanda

I am writing this letter in the hope that I don't have to say this to you in person. Not because I am a coward, but because I cannot bear to see the look of pain in your eyes. I know this letter will not ease the burden, but I hope that it will help where spoken words could not.

With this ring I would have proposed to you on the day we lost our child. I've wanted to give this to you for so long. I leave it for you now in the hope that you will remember happier times.

I wish I could tell you the reason I have to leave, but I cannot. I do not want you to feel that it was your fault, because I know the guilt that you feel over the loss of our child.

Know this, Amanda. What happened wasn't your fault and, despite what you may have thought, I never stopped loving you. And I never will. From the first moment I saw you in that tavern, I knew that I never wanted to be apart from you. It is only because of forces beyond my control that I am to be away from you. But know this. I am doing this to protect you. You were my all, my one, my love.

With this ring, I will always be with you. And I hope you will forgive me.

I love you with all my heart. Be happy. I know that you will always do the right thing when it comes to it.

Love forever,
Wilfred

Chapter 13

Amanda held the letter to her chest, tears streaming down her cheeks. Reading these words was a validation that she could not have wished for. She believed that she had driven Wilfred away and had always cursed herself for it. But what could it have been that made him leave? What could have forced him away from her?

She turned back to the picture of her and Wilfred, overlooking the cot. Looking at the picture of how happy she and Wilfred were, expecting their first child, reminded her of a promise that she once made herself.

She had promised that, when the child was born, she would do anything she could to protect it. When the baby died, she felt as if she had failed. That's why she went to magic for help. All she ever wanted to do was fix that one mistake—because she could not live with the guilt that she felt.

Amanda then looked back at the picture with the words MY NEW BEST FRIEND on it. It made her sad. Daryl needed her help—and she had turned him over to the enemies.

Amanda closed her eyes, feeling new resolve take over. She kissed the ring and placed it in her pocket, reading back the letter once more. She also took the picture that Daryl had drawn for her and pocketed that as well.

I know that you will always do the right thing when it comes to it.

"Come on, Wolvie," Amanda said to the moon wolf, her heart lifted and her self-belief rising once more. "Let's go get Daryl back."

Chapter 14

The Rescue

Castle Gryphenpyre

"Put your backs into it!" Kimera shouted at the servants. "Come on, this needs to be ready before noon!"

The servants worked tirelessly and with little time for a break. A giant stake had been set up in the middle of the courtyard and servants were prepping the bottom of it with firewood, straw and anything that would burn.

"Come on, come on!" Kimera snapped, clapping his hands. "More wood for the fire!"

"There's already enough wood on there," one servant complained to another, fighting to find space. "Why do we need so much of it?"

"Hey, you're not getting paid to talk!" Kimera snapped at the two servants. "Get more wood! I want the whole of Celtland to be able to see this fire."

Chapter 14

The two servants grumbled, moving away to get more wood. "They don't pay us enough to work for that monkeybadger," he whispered to his comrade.

Wrightson

Scarface and Beardy were close to falling asleep at the city entrance. It had been a pretty boring day and they could not wait until the change of shift so that they could get down to the tavern for their afternoon nip. Beardy closed his eyes for a second and was just about to doze off before a figure, wearing a purple hood over their face, came into view with a large dog beside them. Instantly, Beardy and Scarface jumped into action, pointing their pikes towards the visitor. "Who goes there?" Beardy asked.

"I just have some business in Wrightson," the figure said.

"No one goes in or out," Beardy said.

"Unless you pay a toll," Scarface cut in.

The figure pointed at both guards, then moved their fingers together. Scarface and Beardy's heads slammed into each other and they both went down, dazed. The figure then pulled their hood back, revealing her brown and grey hair. "Keep the change."

Wolvie panted in some kind of wolfish laugh. Amanda stroked his head. "Stay close to me, boy."

She cast a spell and she and Wolvie became invisible. They walked past the semi-unconscious guards and into the city. Technically there was no need to knock them out—but Amanda figured that she'd have to tangle with the guards of Wrightson at some point, so she wanted the practice. Not only that, but she also wanted some payback from the way those guards treated her earlier.

Moments after Amanda had made her way into the city, two more guards arrived. "All right, lads. Change of guard."

Upon seeing Scarface and Beardy on the ground, they panicked. "What happened?"

"A woman . . . ," Scarface mumbled. "A woman . . . and a dog . . ."

"Go tell the Captain!" one of them cried.

The guard ran back into the city as fast as his legs could carry him, heading towards the barracks in search of his captain. However, he found Luthar, not at the barracks as expected, but outside a tavern, face down on a table and with at least three empty ale mugs in front of him. He looked a mess and the guard felt a little apprehensive to wake him. But he ran up to Luthar and shook him. "Captain! Captain!"

Luthar grunted and raised his head, his beard soaked with alcohol. "Can't you see I'm busy . . ." He held the side of his face, the ale starting to make him pay for drinking so much.

"Sir!" the guard stammered. "We've been breached, sir!"

"Breached?" Luthar grunted, holding his head. "What are you talking about?"

"The guards at the front are unconscious, sir. They were knocked out."

"Knocked out?" Luthar laughed. "There's no way. I trained these men myself."

"They said it was a woman . . . and a dog . . ."

"A woman knocked those men out? Son . . . I find that hard to . . ." He did a double take. "Wait a minute . . . did you say, a woman *and* a dog?"

"That's what they said, sir."

Luthar pulled himself to his feet, a look of shock on his face.

"Shall I alert the guard, sir?"

"No, son," Luthar replied. "Let me deal with them. Not a word to anyone, you just carry on with your duties. And not a word to *anyone.*" Luthar emphasised that last word as strongly as he could.

"Yes, sir!"

The guard ran off. Luthar stroked his beard thoughtfully, hoping to clear some of the ale that was soaked in it.

Could it be the sorceress? Luthar thought, his hangover clearing. *And the dog must be her wolf. But I thought Kimera killed him?* Then he remembered that this dog was a moon wolf. And the stories went that moon wolves could be healed by the power of moonlight. At least according to the stories his mother told him. *If she is here . . .*

Oh no . . .

Amanda made sure that Wolvie stayed as close to her as possible to maintain the invisibility spell. They walked at a slow pace, despite their urgency. Invisibility magic was a useful spell, but somewhat fickle. It only worked when the user moved without haste. Any act of aggression or sudden movement could break the spell and ruin Amanda's cover. So she had to take her time.

Chapter 14

Amanda felt somewhat nervous walking amongst them, even though she knew they could not see her or Wolvie. She knew that she had to be careful not to connect with anyone as that could also break her spell. So she took her time, carefully making her way through the people and keeping as much distance between them and her as she could.

Ahead, she heard shouting. A group of city residents were running through the town, spreading terrible news that they had heard. "Everyone, the King has announced a burning in the courtyard. The son of Queen Sheena has been found. And they're going to burn him!"

The word spread quickly as the city folk gossiped. Some were horrified, others didn't believe it—but all of them wanted to see for themselves. They stopped what they were doing and ran towards the direction of the courtyard. Amanda suddenly saw a surge of them heading towards her, so she had to pull Wolvie to one side and rest against a wall to let them pass. The crowd of people stampeded by and the street was empty in seconds.

Only then did Amanda allow herself to be horrified at the news. "He's . . . going to burn Daryl?"

Were there no depths that this King would sink? Daryl was only a child. Then Amanda remembered that it was *she* that handed Daryl to Kimera, so she had put him in this situation. If Daryl died, it would be on her conscience. She was not prepared to let that happen.

"We got to get moving, Wolvie," Amanda whispered.

Picking up the pace, but not so much that she didn't break her invisibility spell, she and Wolvie continued forward.

A lone chicken walked out of a cage from a nearby stall. The trader had not properly reinforced it and was halfway through fixing it before the news spread. This chicken wandered in front of them and accidentally bumped into the invisible Wolvie, causing the wolf to growl instinctively. The chicken, startled by the bodiless noise, started to cluck loudly and shake its wings.

"Ssshhhh!" Amanda hissed, worried that the chicken's noise would attract too much attention. "Please be quiet."

But the chicken clucked and waived its wings violently, thinking it was under attack. The noise carried across the empty street. Amanda begging the chicken didn't help—so instead she had to take more drastic measures. She jumped on top of the chicken, grabbing it and trying to cover its beak with her hands. The chicken snapped and bit at her as Amanda wrestled with the animal, squawking louder than before.

"Hey! Hold still will you!"

Amanda's hands were bleeding a little from the chicken's bite, but she eventually got a good grasp of it, placing her hands around the chicken's neck. "Ha! Got you now!"

"Ahem!"

Amanda's eyebrows raised. She turned round, noticing four heavily armed guards behind her. Looking down, she saw that her body was no longer invisible. In her haste to keep the chicken silent, she had forgotten that physical contact broke the spell.

"Er, hey," Amanda said, smiling sheepishly. "How's it going?"

"What have we got here?" the tallest guard asked, the end of his metal cudgel tapping the palm of his left hand.

Amanda's eyes darted between the guards and the chicken whilst she tried to think of a valid excuse.

"Um . . . I just felt like . . . choking the chicken . . ."

Really, Amanda? she thought. *That's the best you could come up with?*

She let the chicken go and it ran away, squawking down the street.

Amanda stood up; Wolvie growled at her side. She wished that she could activate her invisibility spell again—unfortunately invisibility magic required a long recharge time.

"Looks like we got a witch amongst us, boys," the tallest guard said.

"Er, I don't know what you are talking about," Amanda said.

"People don't just disappear and reappear like that," the tallest guard growled.

"She's clearly a witch!" another of the guards said behind her.

"We don't take kindly to your type here," another said.

The guards advanced, cudgels in hand. Just one of them looked like it could break every bone in Amanda's body. And judging by their sneering expressions, they didn't look like they were about to be gentlemanly to her.

"Er, say now . . . ," Amanda stammered. "Um, maybe we just got off on the wrong foot . . . how about we, er . . ." She had an idea. "How about we—kiss and make up?"

She went through the motion of blowing a kiss to them, using both hands. But she exerted a little more lung power in her exhale, sending a wind that knocked the guards over.

Chapter 14

"Oh and, one more thing," Amanda sniggered. "I prefer the term sorceress."

"Get her!"

The guards got to their feet and charged at her. With several waves of her hands, Amanda used her psychokinesis magic to toss them aside, one by one, into the brick wall, knocking them all out. Amanda stood with her arms folded, feeling somewhat empowered that she was able to take out four men that were about 200 pounds heavier than her.

"No problem," she said. She cracked her knuckles as if to demonstrate how tough she was. "Ow!" She shook her hand.

As much fun as she had beating up those bullies, Amanda remembered her mission. "Wolvie, we have to go, now."

Wolvie nodded and they turned round to rush down the street.

They stopped when they saw a lone guard ahead of them, his green cape billowing in the wind.

"I know why you're here," Luthar said. "And I'm telling you—turn away now."

Amanda recognised this man from the first time she arrived at the city. "It's Luthar, right? Please just let us pass; we've come here to save Daryl."

Luthar drew his sword. "I can't let you do that."

Amanda held her nerve. Wolvie stood to attention, ready to pounce at a moment's notice. But Amanda sensed the hesitation in Luthar's voice and she guessed that he didn't want to be here. "I've

already taken out six of your guards," she threatened. "And I can just as easily take you out as well." She backed off her tone. "But, I can see that you're a good man. You looked after us when we first came to Wrightson. I don't want to fight you."

"Neither do I," Luther replied ruefully. "But my duty is to the King."

"The King? You can't honestly tell me that you're happy taking orders from him?"

"Of course I'm not!" Luthar roared. "I hate that man and everything he has forced me to do. But I swore an oath to serve the Crown."

"How can you say that?" Amanda asked, exasperated. "He burned down Daryl's village."

Luthar closed his eyes, his heart heavy in his chest. "I know. He made me give the order. My hands are just as stained with blood as his. People have died and . . . I have done nothing." He sheathed his sword. "I am as guilty for those deaths as he is." He held out his arms in a form of surrender. "Do what you must. I am ready."

"Ready?"

"To face my punishment."

"I'm . . . I'm not going to kill you."

"Please . . . Burn me. Freeze me. Rip me to pieces. ANYTHING! Please! I'm begging you . . . I can't . . . I . . ." Tears formed in Luthar's eyes. "I don't . . . want to live . . . with this guilt . . . anymore . . ."

He fell to his knees, placing his hands over his eyes and wept. Amanda felt so sorry for him, a man of his standing, reduced to this. But she was not about to kill him. Instead, she walked over to him and knelt down. Placing a hand over his shoulder, she spoke calmly to him, understanding his pain. "I know about living with guilt. I've also learned that, if you let it consume you, it drives you away from everyone and everything you care about. But you don't have to let it consume you. You can do something about it."

"What . . . can I do?" Luthar cried. "I'm beyond redemption."

"No one is beyond redemption," Amanda told him. "You just have to want it."

Luthar looked up at Amanda. She smiled back at him. The words that she had said really struck a chord with him. Could he make up for six years of evil?

Chapter 14

But then, if this woman, who he had only known for just a day, had faith in him, maybe there was a chance.

Sheena. I will avenge you.

"He will be burning Daryl in the courtyard very soon," Luthar said. "We have to be fast."

Amanda smiled.

"Just promise me one thing," Luthar requested. "Let me have Kimera!"

"He's all yours!" Amanda agreed.

Luthar got to his feet. "The entrance to the courtyard will be too heavily guarded and the amount of people will block our entrance. But I know a back way in, through the battlements overlooking the courtyard. He won't expect an attack from above."

"Let's do it," Amanda said.

"We don't have time to waste," Luthar said. "Oh and, thank you, sorceress."

"Call me Amanda."

Chapter 15

Payback

Castle Gryphenpyre

The people of the city pushed in as far as they could, almost surging forward. A unit of guards kept them back so that they could not get too close. Every single one of them wanted to see what was happening, having heard the news spread across the city. Last minute adjustments were being made to the stake with pitch being thrown down to make the fire spread faster.

The sun finally reached its zenith, signalling noon. It was time.

A row of trumpeters played a fanfare and, stepping out into the courtyard, Kimera and a procession of guards followed. He waived to the crowd, smiling at them and giving false thanks to them all. The crowd made no reaction—they were too angry to cheer him, but too afraid to boo him. The fanfare continued as Kimera made

127

his way a few feet in front of the stake. He cleared his throat. "My loyal subjects . . ."

Another fanfare blazed before the King spoke, interrupting him. Every time the King tried to speak, the fanfare interrupted him, going on longer than it should have been. After three attempts, Kimera could wait no longer. "OH SHUT UP!"

The fanfare went silent.

"That's better. Ahem. My loyal subjects. Today is a great day for all of Celtland. For today, we celebrate what is to be my greatest victory. And I wanted you all to share in this precious moment . . ."

From the battlements above, Luthar, Amanda and Wolvie watched, crouching down low. Just as Luthar expected, Kimera had ordered all the guards to hold back the crowd, leaving the battlements unattended. It meant that they were able to sneak on top of it without being noticed. They kept low whilst Kimera spoke. He seemed to speak for a long time, a lot of it utter nonsense and seemingly just for the sake of it. It wasn't long before Amanda and Luthar were bored out of their skulls.

"This man likes the sound of his own voice a little too much," Amanda yawned.

"You're telling me," Luthar agreed.

Kimera continued with his speech. His very, very long speech.

". . . and so, it was on that fateful day that, six years ago, I—Kimera Gryphenpyre—became your King. Your perfect, wonderful King."

He waited for a response from the crowd, only to see most of them were fast asleep. Somewhat embarrassed, he signalled to the trumpeters. "Play something!"

The trumpeters played a quick burst to wake the crowd up. Everyone jumped.

"And now, without further ado," Kimera cried, "I bring you to our main event of the afternoon. Bring forth the prisoner!"

"Let me go!"

"Daryl!" Amanda gasped.

Daryl was pulled into the courtyard, dragged by a couple of guards on either side, pulling him in view of the crowd. The crowd gasped upon seeing him.

"This, my people, is Daryl Gryphenpyre. Son of Queen Sheena Gryphenpyre. Many of you have been spreading rumours of this boy's existence, and I think it's only fair that I confirm it to be true.

And yes, many of you also know that he is technically next in line to the throne of Celtland. But look at him, he's just a boy. And do you all really want a boy ruling you over a man that has experience?"

"Long live King Daryl!"

A cry rose up from the crowd—a brave soul, in a moment of light, speaking his mind. Another voice spoke up, echoing the same. And then another. And another. And another.

"Long live King Daryl!"
"Long live King Daryl!"
"Long live King Daryl!"
"Long live King Daryl!"
"Long live King Daryl!"

Soon, *everyone* in the crowd was chanting, something that Kimera did not expect. Hearing this, Daryl smiled. He hadn't even met most of these people, but already they were taking to him—just by being the son of their most beloved Queen.

"Stop that," Kimera stammered. "Please . . . make them stop!"

The guards did everything they could to try and silence them, but the crowd would not be silenced. They cheered their support of Daryl.

"Be quiet!" Kimera said. "Be quiet!"

From above, Amanda smiled. It was great that Kimera was squirming and that the crowd was telling him what they really thought of his rule. He seemed to be losing control, until his rage got the better of him.

"SHUT UP!"

Kimera's lion roar silenced the crowd. Now he was back in control.

"You forget your place. I AM KING! And no one, even this little runt here, will take it from me! Tie him to the stake!"

The guards pulled Daryl as he squirmed and bit at their arms, nearly breaking his teeth on their armour. They dragged him towards the stake and tied him to it. Whilst this was going on, an executioner, wearing a black mask, stepped forward, carrying a torch. On seeing the fire, Daryl shook in terror, wriggling frantically to try and break the ropes holding him.

"We have to do something!" Amanda cried, unable to sit back and watch any further.

Luthar nodded in agreement. "Any ideas?"

Chapter 15

"We deal with the fire first," Amanda said. "Then we go down there and rescue Daryl."

"So, we just go down there, fight all the heavily armed guards and just rescue Daryl?" Luthar asked, a little sardonic. "For a second there, I was worried you'd come up with something suicidal."

Once Daryl was secured, the guards moved away. Kimera turned back to the crowd with a sneer. "Let this be a warning to everyone who dares think they can oppose my will," Kimera warned them. "Remember, I am your King, whether you like it or not."

He nodded towards the executioner, who moved closer and put the torch towards the wood near the stake.

"You both may want to stand back," Amanda warned Luthar and Wolvie. They didn't take this threat lightly and did as they were told. Amanda held up her hands and cold air began to swirl around her hands, which enlarged into a massive ball of frozen air.

The pitch that covered the stake caused the fire to spread quickly around Daryl. The people were aghast as the flames lit up. Daryl screamed as the flames licked around him.

"If you see my sister," Kimera smirked at Daryl, "Tell her that her little brother says hi!"

Amanda blew at the ball of ice, using her wind magic to carry it the extra distance. The ball of ice struck the wood surrounding the stake, turning it white as snow and instantly negating the heat. The flame vanished before any of it touched Daryl.

"What in the name of the dragons?" Kimera cursed, confused.

Luthar drew his sword. "Guess it's now or never!"

He leapt over the battlements, grabbing onto the long banner that dangled almost all the way to the bottom. As he reached the end, he pushed off the wall, letting go and spinning round in the air, landing in the most dramatic way he could muster.

Wolvie did likewise, gliding down the banner, pushing off near the end and doing a double spin in the air before landing on all his paws.

Seeing her friends do this, Amanda wanted a piece of the action. *Piece of cake.*

She jumped over the edge, grabbing onto the banner like Luthar had done. Unfortunately, the rough material burned her hands as she slid down (Luthar made it look so easy) and when she pushed off near the end, she flailed around, which threw her off balance.

"Oh . . . RATS!"

She tumbled down, landing into a cart of hay.

Everyone turned to the cart, waiting for Amanda to show herself. A second later, she burst forth, slightly dazed. "I'm okay!" She stumbled out of the cart, shaking her head from side to side.

"What is the meaning of this?" Kimera shouted, shocked. "Luthar? What do you think you're doing?"

"What I should have done six years ago!" Luthar growled.

"Guards!" Kimera shouted.

The guards that were holding the crowd back held their ground. More guards poured out into the courtyard, armed and ready.

"Seize them!"

The guards ran to attack, but Luthar was ready. He had trained most of these guards himself, so he knew how to take them. He did not want to kill any of them, as he knew that they were only doing their jobs, so he just disarmed them instead.

Amanda and Wolvie rushed towards Daryl. She used her magic to knock back any guard that came her way. Wolvie jumped from guard to guard, biting and scratching them.

"Stop them!" Kimera squealed, jumping up and down like a spoilt child. "Stop them, you idiots!"

But the guards proved to be useless as Luthar, Amanda and Wolvie alone took them out. Amanda and Wolvie reached Daryl with little problem. Wolvie ran up behind the stake and bit into the ropes, using his sharp claws to free him.

"Wolvie! You're alive!" Daryl cried. Once he was free, he embraced his pet. Wolvie whined happily.

"Daryl," Amanda said, somewhat nervously. She didn't know how Daryl would react to seeing her again.

"Amanda?" Daryl gasped. "You . . . came back for me."

"Of course I did."

"What . . . what about your reward?"

Amanda knelt down, placing a hand to the side of Daryl's face. "You're the only reward that I need," she said tearfully. "Daryl, I was wrong. I should have never given you away to Kimera."

Kimera was now in hysterics. "Guards! Get Daryl, get Daryl!"

Guards swarmed in on Daryl, but Amanda stood in front of him, hands alight with magic. "Anyone who wants to take him will have to go through me first!"

Chapter 15

The guards held their ground nervously. Seeing how easily Amanda took out their comrades, neither of them were particularly keen to attack her. But their King's commands rang in their ear.

"Don't just stand there, take them!"

"No!"

This time it was Luthar's roar that silenced everyone.

"Kimera! This ends now! I challenge you to a duel!"

"A . . . duel . . . ? But, I am your King!"

"You were never my King," Luthar roared. "You murdered the woman I loved! You forced me to spill innocent blood! No more! It ends *today*!"

Kimera's moment of panic disappeared after a few seconds. "You forget, I can choose *not* to accept a duel, as long as I name another champion. And I have plenty of guards that are willing to fall on a sword for me. Who will be my champion?"

Kimera looked around. No guard took up the offer, nor did any dare look him in the eye. "I said, who will be my champion?"

"You have no more followers, Kimera," Luthar snarled. "Now face me like a man."

Kimera started shaking. Luthar was one of the meanest soldiers in all of Celtland. This man had been fighting wars pretty much as soon as he was able to stand—and whilst Kimera had also fought in wars, he hadn't fought in *nearly* as many as Luthar had. But Kimera knew that he couldn't look weak in front of his people. Not if people expected to take him seriously as King.

"Give me a sword!" he shouted.

"Give him a weapon," Luthar said. A guard obeyed and threw the King a weapon. It landed at his feet. Kimera was shocked that this guard threw him one without handing it to him.

"Pick it up," Luthar challenged.

Kimera carefully bent down (something that was hard to do with his large belly) and took the sword in both hands. It had been awhile since he had lifted one of these and the weapon felt a little heavy in his hands. "You . . . you think I'm scared of you?" Kimera challenged.

"No," Luthar cried. "I think you're terrified."

"Go get him, Luthar!" Daryl called out.

Luthar circled Kimera, watching him closely. He saw that Kimera was nervous as he didn't have a strong hold of his blade and his grip was shaky. Not to mention that he was sweating and his palms were greasy and wet. This fight wouldn't last long.

With a roar, Luthar charged at Kimera, swinging his sword. Kimera only just got his weapon up in time to defend himself, blocking Luthar's attacks. Amanda and Daryl cheered encouragement as Luthar fought bravely, whilst Kimera cowered in fear at his opponent's fearsome attacks. There was no way that Kimera could match Luthar—he was too strong for him.

Luthar's blade lightly nipped at Kimera's hand, drawing blood. Kimera squealed and pulled his hand back. With one less grip on the sword, Luthar slammed his blade into Kimera's, knocking it out of his hand. Luthar then punched him in the face, breaking his nose, and kneed him in the belly before pushing him down.

"Oooh, he's going to be sore tomorrow," Amanda chuckled.

Luthar held his blade to Kimera's neck. Kimera, his nose running with his own blood, held out his hands as if begging for mercy. "Luthar, stop!"

"Now I have you, worm!"

"Please . . . You don't have to do this. I . . . I . . . I'll give you anything you want if you let me live."

"You have nothing that I want!"

"Luthar, please! I know I made you do some horrible things and I killed my sister. I can't take back what I made you do. But, Luthar . . . you're a man of honour. You wouldn't kill a man in cold blood, would you?"

Luthar held the blade nearer Kimera's neck. One move would be all it would take to end it. Kimera would be finished. The world would be a safer place. Everything would be safe once again in the world of Celtland. Kimera held his breath, waiting for Luthar's answer.

"No," Luthar said, lowering his sword. "I wouldn't. Because unlike you, I am not a murderer."

He reached down, grabbed Kimera by the hand and lifted him to his feet. "I *am* a man of honour and that's what separates you from me. I'll see to it that you live out your sins in prison. Maybe you can find some redemption for your sins."

"You think so?" Kimera asked.

Luthar turned and looked back to Amanda. "As an old friend once said, no one is past redemption—if they want it."

Amanda smiled back at Luthar.

Chapter 15

"Thank you, Luthar," Kimera sniffed, keeping one hand behind his back. "I am so glad that you are an honourable man."

He took the handle of the dagger attached to his belt. "Then again, honour is for the weak!"

"Look out!" Amanda cried.

Too late! Kimera's dagger drove into Luthar's neck—the one part of his armour that was unguarded. Luthar gasped and staggered, clutching his wound. He took a few steps and fell to his knees. Amanda, Daryl and Wolvie ran to his side.

"You idiot!" Kimera shouted. "You think I want *redemption*? I don't need to be redeemed—I am KING! And when you are King, you don't need an excuse for what you do. You do it because you can! Because no one can stop you! Because the whole world revolves around you!"

Amanda checked the wound on Luthar's neck. It was a deep wound, but Amanda was sure that she could fix it if she applied her magic soon enough. "Hold still."

She waved a hand over the wound and her magic worked—but this was a fatal wound and it would take a lot longer to heal, assuming Luthar didn't die before.

"Now that I've proven my worth—guards, arrest that woman and bring me Daryl!"

The guards were reluctant to obey his orders, but Kimera had proven his strength by beating Luthar in battle, albeit through questionable means. They advanced towards Daryl and Amanda.

"I am sorry . . . My King," Luthar apologised weakly to Daryl. "I . . . failed you . . ."

"Don't speak like that," Amanda said. "You did your best."

"But, it wasn't good enough," Luthar replied. "It's up to you now, Amanda."

"Me?" Amanda gasped. "But, what can I do?"

"You came all the way here to rescue Daryl," Luthar told her. "You wouldn't have done it if you didn't care for the boy. Please . . . protect my son."

"You . . . you're my dad?" Daryl gasped.

Luthar turned back to the boy, saying words that he had wanted to say for so long. "I loved your mother," Luthar replied. "But I could not protect her. I'm so sorry . . ."

He turned back to Amanda. "Do what I could not."

Amanda's gaze moved towards Daryl, the cute little six-year-old that came into her life and brought light where there was darkness. His frightened little face sent tremors down her spine. And the thought of him being stuck with that monster Kimera was too much for her to face.

Squeezing her eyes shut and clenching her fists, she turned round to the King and exclaimed, "Kimera! I challenge you to a duel!"

The courtyard went silent. Kimera's eyebrows raised in shock. He then burst into laughter. "YOU?!? Challenging *me* to a duel?"

"Let's call it a Winner Take All match," Amanda challenged. "I beat you and you surrender your crown to Daryl."

"And when I beat you?" Kimera asked.

Amanda sighed hard. "You get to take Daryl."

"Forget it," Kimera snarled. "Why should I fight for him when I could just take him here and now?"

"What's the matter? Scared you'll lose to a girl?"

A hushed gasp came from the crowd who were still watching from the sidelines. Kimera sneered at Amanda, but at the same time impressed by the courage she displayed. "I underestimated you. Very well, I will accept. On one condition. You don't use any magic."

"No . . . magic . . . ?" Amanda hadn't expected that.

"You've proven yourself to be quite the little hell-raiser with your magic," Kimera said. "But let's see how powerful you are *without* it. Unless of course, you don't think you can take me?"

"I can take you, magic or no magic," Amanda accepted without a moment's hesitation.

"Amanda, no," Daryl said.

"Trust me," Amanda said, looking back. She bent down to pick up Luthar's sword. "I'm gonna need to borrow this."

"Be my guest . . . ," Luthar agreed.

She took Luthar's sword in both hands and stood up. "Okay, Kimera, let's go!" She lifted up the sword, but the blade turned out to be heavier than she imagined and she fell backwards, landing quite hard on her backside, much to the amusement of Kimera.

"My bad," Amanda said, getting back to her feet, smiling but embarrassed.

"Have you ever used a sword before?" Luthar asked.

"What? Me? Oh yeah, sure," Amanda replied. "I use swords all the time!"

"You've never picked one up, have you?"

Chapter 15

"No . . . never. But I've seen others use it—how hard can it be?"

We're finished, thought Luthar.

Kimera picked up his own sword and the two started circling each other. Amanda, having underestimated how heavy swords could be, dragged her sword along the ground, only able to lift it up for a few moments at a time.

"Well," Kimera sneered. "Ladies first."

"Okay, you asked for it!" Amanda cried. She lifted up her sword and swung it at Kimera, but he easily moved back to avoid it. The weight of the weapon forced her to spin round and she tripped over herself, landing flat on her face. *That was embarrassing.*

"Okay, that was a practice one," Amanda said, getting back to her feet. "This one is for real."

She charged at Kimera and swung the sword. This time he stepped to one side and again, Amanda fell face down, much to the laughter of all the guards.

"You're doing great, Amanda," Daryl cried. "Don't give up."

Well at least I got a vote of confidence, Amanda thought.

"Keep your feet still when you swing it," Luthar cried. "That'll help you bear the weight."

"Feet still, got it," Amanda said. Quickly getting up, she turned to face Kimera. Taking the advice she was given, Amanda kept her feet still, swinging the weapon at the King. She was able to take the weight this time, but her swings were somewhat lacklustre as she had still not gotten used to the weight of the weapon. Kimera simply sidestepped each strike by stepping back, hardly using any effort at all to avoid the attacks. He didn't even raise his sword.

After awhile, he put a hand to his mouth and yawned. "This really is quite embarrassing, you know."

A final swing from Amanda cut the skin open from Kimera's hand as he put it to his face to yawn. Kimera yelped and pulled his hand back. Blood trickled from where Amanda had struck him.

"Yeah! You go Amanda!" Daryl cried.

Amanda was quite pleased with herself, so she allowed herself a smirk. "Not bad for a beginner, eh?"

Kimera took his weapon in both hands, snarling. "That's it! I was playing around with you before, but that ends now!"

Kimera charged at Amanda. She sidestepped, swinging her sword round and hitting him on the backside with the flat end, causing

Kimera to yelp in pain. The crowd laughed as Amanda humiliated the King. Even Daryl allowed himself a chuckle.

"Stop it! Stop laughing at me!"

With his pride (and his bottom) hurt, Kimera redoubled his efforts against Amanda, lifting his sword as he tried another charge. But Amanda was ready for him. As he brought the sword down, Amanda moved to one side and, with a spare leg, kicked the King in the backside. As he crashed, the land around him rumbled like a mini earthquake. The crowd cheered and laughed again. Amanda even did a little showboating for the crowd. It was nice to have a crowd that cheered for her for a change instead of wanting to kick her out of town.

"You're doing well, Amanda," Luthar cried, actually impressed that she was picking this up so quickly. "Stay on him!"

"Don't worry," Amanda cried, turning back to Kimera. He was struggling to get to his feet, seemingly having trouble due to his wide girth. Seeing him at his weakest, Amanda decided to press the attack. "I got this one."

She ran to him, raising the sword above.

"No, Amanda! Stop!"

But Amanda was so overconfident in her attack that she didn't listen to Luthar's warning. As she got within a few inches of Kimera, he turned round whilst still kneeling.

And Amanda felt a sharp pain rip through her stomach.

"NO!" Daryl cried.

The crowd went silent.

Amanda looked down and saw Kimera's sword in her stomach.

"You idiot," Kimera laughed. "You fell for the oldest trick in the book." He pulled the sword from her. "And now you're dead."

Amanda stumbled back a few feet, dropped her own weapon and then fell to her knees. She clutched her wound, the blood flowing from her as she struggled to breathe. The pain that ran through her was greater than anything she had ever felt in her life.

"Amanda!"

Amanda looked up, seeing Daryl's worried face. Wolvie let out a small whine. Even Luthar looked horrified.

I . . . I can heal myself . . . the Blood gem . . .

NO! I can't. Never again . . .

"Daryl," she said, tears in her eyes. "I'm so sorry . . ."

Daryl started to cry. Wolvie looked at her with a sad look as well.

Chapter 15

"I suppose you may as well know something before you die," Kimera said. "Your boyfriend, William . . . was it? No . . . Wilson . . . Wil . . . Wilfred, that was it! He came to us just after your attack in your hometown. Everyone in the town wanted to have you strung up and executed for what you did. But he begged for your life. I listened to him of course and decided to grant his wish, being the merciful type that I am. The only condition was that he leave you and never see you again. He fulfilled his part of the bargain and we spared your life.

"*His* life, however, was a different story."

Hearing this, Amanda turned round, disbelief in her eyes.

"Poor fool never saw it coming," Kimera sniggered. "Forests can be so dangerous. You never know who may leap out at you. Well, an example had to be made for your actions. But, if it's any consolation—he never stopped loving you. He told us that himself.

"Now you can go see him. And don't worry about Daryl. You'll see him soon enough."

Amanda's mind raced upon hearing this. For so long, she had believed herself responsible for pushing Wilfred away—but it was Kimera that took him from her. He was responsible for all her self-loathing and hatred. *Him.* It always had been him.

And now Daryl was at his mercy after she had sworn to protect him.

Amanda felt all the rage inside her build up—a rage she had tried to keep down. Because if she gave into it, the monster would arise.

When she looked up and saw the guards advancing on Daryl her rage became stronger. It would not be silenced. Not anymore.

Him . . . it was all him.

I . . . I can't give in . . .

No . . . let it go. Why hold back?

Do it for Daryl.

Save him.

Let it go . . .

Let it go . . .

Let . . .

It . . .

GO!!!

Amanda's eyes turned blood red. An aura of red energy surrounded her. The wound healed instantly.

She lifted back her head, stood up and let out a terrible roar as the red energy around her exploded like a volcano. The rage that she had tried to keep back was finally let loose.

And with it—the monster was free!

She turned to Kimera, her eyes devoid of mercy, kindness or anything else that made her human. When she spoke, her voice was no longer hers—it was the voice of an uncaged beast.

"KIMERA! YOU'RE MINE!"

Kimera trembled in fear, nearly dropping the weapon in his hand. Amanda stomped towards him like an enraged giant, every step was like an explosion, a meteor hitting the ground with full fury. "Stay back!" he cried, holding up his sword. "Stay back!"

"Try it again!" Amanda roared. "Try it!"

Without even thinking, Kimera thrust the sword at Amanda again, stabbing her in the same place as before. This time, no blood came from the wound. She pulled the sword out from her and bent it out of shape like it was made of rubber, deforming it completely. She didn't even look fazed by the attack from him.

"Guards!" Kimera cried. "Defend me!"

Several guards did as commanded and ran towards Amanda. But one swing of her arm sent them all flying away—it was like Amanda had the strength of a hundred men and these guards were like twigs in her presence. She let out a terrible roar again, a warning to anyone who dared take her on. When she turned back, she saw Kimera running towards the castle—running for his life.

Chapter 15

"You can't run from me," Amanda roared. "I'll hunt you to the ends of Draconica!"

Amanda chased after Kimera, a hunter chasing her prey. It didn't matter where he ran to—she would find him in the end.

Panic took over in the courtyard. People ran away, trying to keep as much distance from Amanda as they could. Luthar was in shock. He turned to Daryl. "What . . . what happened?"

"It must be that gem that Amanda told me about," Daryl replied. "The . . . Blood gem I think it was?"

"Blood gem?" Luthar gasped. "I had no idea those things still existed. But . . . if this is the case, then we are in trouble."

"Why?" Daryl asked. "What's happened to Amanda?"

"I only heard about Blood gems in stories," Luthar explained. "They were used during the Age of Sorcery. Legend states it gave the user superhuman strength and made them virtually indestructible—but at the cost of their sanity."

"Oh no," Daryl cried. "We have to help her."

"We have to get you to safety, My King," Luthar said.

"No! I'm not leaving Amanda! We have to help her, we can't just leave her."

Luthar could see the dedication this boy had to Amanda. She must have been a strong protector for him if he was prepared to speak for her. But a Blood gem was a powerful force—one that even Luthar wasn't sure that they could control. But they would try.

"Very well," Luthar said. "I will accompany you and keep you—argh!"

He tried to stand, but his wound was not fully healed yet and he only stood up a few feet before he was forced down on his knees again. "Go, I'll be okay! I'll follow you in a minute."

Daryl nodded. He and Wolvie ran after Amanda, hoping to catch up to her. Luthar just hoped that they could get to Amanda in time and help her. Because if they didn't, what happened in Ashfeld would seem like a bonfire in comparison.

A piece of paper blew in front of Daryl and brushed against his face. He grabbed it and looked at it, his eyes widening in surprise. It was the picture he drew of Amanda, him and Wolvie. He remembered drawing this back at her house. It was one of his favourite pictures that he had ever drawn. But there was no way this picture could have come this far unless . . . Amanda had brought it with her.

Chapter 16

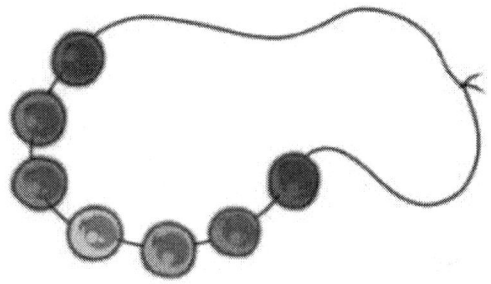

The Sorceress's Pain

Castle Gryphenpyre

Kimera puffed and panted as he struggled to keep moving. Amanda was in hot pursuit behind him. His legs struggled to maintain his own weight as he forced himself ahead. He cursed his heavy girth, having gained extra weight through heavy feasting over his years as King. If he survived this, he would make sure that he did more exercise.

He looked behind him. Amanda was still after him, matching him every step of the way. She was like a hungry wolf out for blood. His blood.

Kimera charged towards the entrance to the castle, running through the open gates.

"CLOSE THE GATES!" he cried as he ran through.

Chapter 16

Seconds later, the creaking sound of the metal gate was heard as the servants activated the mechanism to close it. The closing of the gate seemed to take longer than Kimera had hoped and he could see Amanda was closing in on him quicker.

"CLOSE IT!" he cried. "CLOSE IT! CLOSE IT!"

Amanda was getting closer and closer now and the gate didn't seem like it would be shut in time. But just as Amanda was about to cross the threshold, the gate slammed shut.

Kimera breathed a sigh of relief and allowed himself a moment to catch his breath. There was no way Amanda could get to him now. That gate was twenty tonnes of solid iron. Knowing he was safe, Kimera allowed a moment to gloat. "There!" he panted. "Try and get me now!"

The gate creaked and shook as a force outside banged against it. A fist-sized hole appeared in it. Then another, then another, and then another, until: *CRACK!*

A section in the door burst out and Kimera saw Amanda looking right at him, her hands resting on either side of the hole.

"Peek-a-boo . . . I see you."

Kimera gasped aloud. He screamed as Amanda ripped the door in two, tearing it in half like it was paper. Twenty tonnes of solid iron—and Amanda tore it apart like it was nothing.

"I told you that there was nowhere in the world that you could go where I could not find you."

Kimera turned and ran away again. "GUARDS! PROTECT ME!"

The guards that were on patrol around the castle heard their King's cry and armed themselves against Amanda. Seeing Amanda tear the door down so easily, they did not want to confront her face to face. They armed themselves with crossbows, placing a bolt on them and aiming them straight at her. Lining up and kneeling down, they took aim and fired.

The bolts flew towards Amanda, each of them trained on her and guaranteed not to miss.

Amanda held up her hand and the bolts stopped where they were several inches from her—then dropped to the ground.

Shocked, the guards quickly tried to reload for a second attack, but Amanda stampeded towards them. She sent all of them flying, charging through them like they were nothing more than a minor obstacle. Amanda was somewhat disappointed. No one was giving her a fight worthy of her power.

The Sorceress's Pain

Kimera.

She hadn't lost sight of her target. She could smell his fear, smell his blood.

It would not be long before she tasted his.

Kimera ran up the winding stairs as fast as he could, his legs begging for a break. He didn't care where he was going—he just wanted to get as far away from Amanda as he could. That woman was a monster—he had never seen anyone with that much power before. Where was it coming from? How could she have so much power? He only thought of her as a weak young woman. What had he created?

He eventually ran out onto the battlements of the castle, but could only manage a few more feet before the cramp in his legs finally gave way and he collapsed. He could run no more. Panic stricken, he looked back at the entrance, knowing that it was only a matter of time before Amanda caught up with him. No matter how far he ran, Amanda would catch up with him.

But he didn't want to die. He didn't *deserve* to die, he believed. What had he really done that was so bad? He just wanted to rule the kingdom in the way he believed it should be ruled.

Catching his breath, he reached out for something to help pull him up. His hand rested on smooth iron as opposed to stone. Turning to his side, his eyes widened when he saw his hand resting on the battlement cannons, pointing out towards the open field. Next to it was a pile of unused cannon balls and a tinderbox. And Kimera also noted that the fuse was brand new.

He had to laugh in joy. Fate had been kind to him, providing this wonderful contraption, a marvel of The Age of Science. Kimera had seen these things turn entire legions to mush. Surely there was no way that Amanda could survive it.

Grunting and groaning, Kimera turned the cannon towards the doorway. It wasn't easy moving this thing, usually it took about two people to move it properly, and he nearly ruptured his back in moving it. Once the nozzle was pointing towards where it should have been, he loaded one of the cannonballs into it. By the time he was done, his gown was soaked with sweat. This was more work than he often did in a week.

"Kimera!"

Chapter 16

Amanda's voice echoed from the doorway and Kimera knew that his time was short. Having a last minute check to make sure the cannon was in place, he grabbed one of the tinderboxes, fumbling to open it. The flint dropped onto the floor and Kimera had a sudden panic as he scoured the floor for it. He could hear Amanda's thunderous steps as she made her way up to the battlements—she wasn't even trying to hide her arrival now.

Joy overtook him when he found the flint and he instantly started striking it across the steel to spark the fuse. His hands shook and he could not keep them steady enough, so the flame he created was weak at best.

"Come on, come on!"

He had almost worn the flint through numerous attempts to light it before his last attempt created a spark that made the fuse burn. The sparkle was a delight for Kimera to witness.

Amanda walked onto the battlements, and Kimera could barely hide his smirk. He refused to show her fear, knowing that she would be out of his life in seconds.

"You have nowhere to run now, Kimera," Amanda snarled.

"Run?" Kimera laughed. "I don't have to run when I have this!"

The fuse burned out. The cannon's *BOOM!* echoed throughout the Celtland sky. It was louder than Kimera anticipated and he had to cover his ears from the noise. The cannonball flew towards Amanda.

She held out her finger and the ball stopped mid-flight. Kimera's eyes raised in terror as cracks appeared in the ball before it broke into several pieces.

With the same hand, Amanda opened her fingers as if to grab something. The cannon floated in the air before Kimera, like it was light as a feather. She squeezed her hands. The cannon was crushed into a ball no larger than Kimera's head, and then landed on the ground before Kimera with a thump.

"I ripped through your steel door," Amanda growled. "I knocked aside your guards—and you thought that *this* would destroy me? Your petty toys are no match for the power of sorcery!"

Kimera's heart dropped and the lump in his throat seized up as Amanda walked closer, the red mist in her eyes still burning.

It wasn't hard for Daryl and Wolvie to keep up with Amanda. All they had to do was follow the trail of destruction that she had left.

The Sorceress's Pain

They now arrived at the castle—shocked by the amount of damage that had been done. Not just the heavy iron gate that had been ripped apart—but also the path of bodies.

The guards that had tried to take out Amanda were lying across the floor, groaning in an untidy heap. Daryl was horrified at what he saw.

"Did . . . Amanda do all this?"

Wolvie let out a light whine.

"We have to find her," Daryl cried. "We have to stop her before she does something terrible."

Daryl pressed on, unable to stop for even a moment. He had to get to Amanda—he couldn't let her turn into a monster. He couldn't.

Not when he knew the good inside her.

"You took him away from me!" Amanda roared. "For a whole year, I thought it was *my* fault that he left me."

Kimera backed away and tripped over himself. He scrabbled across the ground, unable to get to his feet. He really wished he hadn't told Amanda what he had now. "Please . . . I . . . I only did what was right . . ."

"That man . . . was my life," Amanda roared, some traces of humanity shining through. "He was my entire world." The monster resurfaced. "And you took him away from me!"

"Amanda, please!" Kimera begged. "There . . . there's more to the story. I was doing what I was told . . . I . . . I . . . someone wanted to keep you alive. But . . . I had to make an example out of someone because of your actions. Believe me, I was doing what was best—"

Kimera was lifted into the air by an invisible force and pulled towards Amanda. He floated before her as her red eyes gazed into his very soul. "You're nothing more than a speck of dust, Kimera. And I'm here to blow you away."

As if to emphasise her point, she blew a concentrate blast of gale force air towards him. Kimera flew through the air and over the battlements, only just grabbing onto the edge of one in time to stop himself from falling.

His fat fingers stumbled over the smooth rock, unable to get a firm grip on it. He tried to pull himself up, but his arms couldn't support his own weight. He lost his grip and one arm flailed in the air. He looked down, seeing the huge distance between where he was and the ground. Everything looked so tiny from this far up. His heart stopped beating and he lost his voice. His fingers went numb from trying to support himself. And then they gave way.

A blinding pain went through his wrist and he stopped falling, though his arm was nearly wrenched from its socket. He looked back—Amanda was standing over him, holding onto his arm. She lifted him up until he could see her burning red eyes. "Did you honestly think that your death would be so easy?"

"Mercy!" Kimera wept.

Amanda placed a hand over his throat. "Did Daryl's parents beg for mercy when you burned them alive?"

Kimera tried to speak but his voice was constricted by the pressure Amanda had put on his neck. She didn't want to hear his excuses anyway.

She lifted Kimera over her head, holding him by his throat and a leg. Kimera weighed nothing to her, like he was a feather. "I'm going to pull you apart, slowly," she roared. "So that you feel the suffering of everyone that you have hurt! And then . . . you know what I might do next? I might just go after all those other people that wronged me."

The Blood gem was starting to take over and Amanda's voice wasn't her own anymore—she was losing control every second that passed.

"You see, I've been holding back this power for a long time, afraid of what I might do. But you know what? I actually *like* it! So I'm not holding back anymore. It's time the whole of Celtland learned the name Amanda Moonstone!"

"Amanda, stop!"

"Daryl?"

In her excitement of power, Amanda hadn't noticed Daryl and Wolvie running towards her until he called out to her.

"Amanda please, don't kill him," Daryl begged.

"Why not?" Amanda roared. "This man murdered your family!"

"But that doesn't mean that he deserves to die!" Daryl cried back. Wolvie stayed behind Daryl, afraid of Amanda. Daryl showed no fear as he stepped closer to her. "Come on, Amanda. This isn't like you."

"Maybe it is," Amanda roared. "Maybe this is just the side of me that I should have let out a long time ago."

"That's the Blood gem talking, not you. Amanda, you have to stop or it will consume you."

"Why should I stop? What's the point in holding back anymore? All my life I tried to be a good little girl, do the right thing, help people—where did it get me? Then, I make one mistake and everyone punishes me for it! They never understood my pain. They just judged me. No one ever believed in me."

"*I* believe in you!" Daryl shouted back. "Amanda. This isn't you. The Amanda I know is sweet and kind. You care about people, and I care for you."

Daryl lifted up the slightly screwed up piece of paper and held it before Amanda. He pointed towards him and Amanda in the picture and the letters above that read MY NEW BEST FRIEND.

"You're my friend."

Seeing this, Amanda's eyes raised in shock, even though the red mist still burned inside them.

"Please, Amanda," Daryl said, tears in his eyes. "Stop this."

It was then that Amanda remembered a similar time to this, when she first lost control. It was those same four words that reminded Amanda of the man that stood before her when she became the monster.

Wilfred.

He was the man that was able to control her last time. But it wasn't the words alone that quelled her rage, but the way he said them. The same way that Daryl said them to her now.

The words were filled with something stronger than hate. Stronger than even magic. The most powerful and calming force that is worth fighting for.

Love.

Amanda closed her eyes tight, threw Kimera to the ground and placed her hands to her head. She grunted in pain as the red aura spun around her like a tornado. The aura spun faster and faster and Amanda screamed as the tornado of red threatened to swallow her. And then, the tornado vanished.

When she opened her eyes again, they had returned to the same green colour as before. Her voice had also returned to the way it used to be. "Daryl?"

She knelt down and held her arms out to Daryl. "Daryl, it's me. I'm back."

But the child backed away, still unsure if it was the real Amanda.

Chapter 16

"Daryl. You trust me, right?"

He hesitated for a few seconds, tears falling from his eyes. Then he ran into Amanda's arms.

"I trust you."

"I'm all right," Amanda said hugging him, "I'm all right now." After the hug, she gazed into his eyes. "Thanks for not giving up on me."

"You didn't give up on me," Daryl whispered. "You saved me."

Amanda smiled back. "*You* saved *me.*"

"Maybe, we saved each other," Daryl suggested.

"Yeah," Amanda chuckled. She turned to Kimera, who was groaning and wailing. She walked over to him, standing tall. Kimera gasped and scuttled away, but he could only go so far. "It's over, Kimera. You're done. Maybe now you'll have a chance to look back over your life and realise the mistakes you've made." She turned back to Daryl. "Come on, kid. Let's go."

And just like that, Kimera saw his entire legacy fall apart. Everything that he had sacrificed to gain was lost. His work was undone.

He felt for his dagger—the very same that had pierced his sister's abdomen before her fall. *You won't take it away from me!* he thought. *No one will!*

Kimera threw the dagger towards Daryl, aiming straight for his head. One direct hit would be all he needed to secure his inheritance to the Crown. One direct hit.

A bolt struck the dagger, knocking it out of the air before it went anywhere near Daryl and sent it over the battlements. Kimera gasped as his final plan to regain his Kingship fell apart.

Luthar, his wound now fully healed, lifted up the crossbow, smiling. "That weapon won't hurt anyone anymore!" he said. "Kimera. You tried to kill the true King. Last time I checked, that was treason. Guards! Arrest that man!"

He pointed towards Kimera and some guards (that Amanda *hadn't* knocked out) ran towards Kimera and seized him.

"What are you doing?" Kimera cried. "I am your King!"

"Not anymore," Luthar said gleefully. How he had wanted to do this for a long time. "Now that the true King—King Daryl—has returned, I obey him now." He turned to the rightful King. "What say you, My King? What shall we do with the prisoner?"

Chapter 16

Daryl was shocked that Luthar was asking *him* what they should do to Kimera. He looked to Amanda.

"You're the King, Daryl. It's your call."

King. That was something that Daryl never would have expected. He looked towards Kimera, the snivelling, whiny little man looking so pathetic, so weak.

Feeling a great sense of empowerment, Daryl puffed up his chest, pointed to him and then, in as commanding a voice he could manage, "Have him thrown in a dungeon. There he'll remain until he is sorry for his actions."

"Oh, you'll pay for this!" Kimera said as the guards pulled him away. "All of you. You'll all pay! You, you and especially you! I'll make it my mission to make you all suffer!"

Wolvie lifted up his backside to Kimera and let out a massive fart in his general direction. Kimera grimaced at the terrible smell. The guards removed Kimera from sight.

"My King," Luthar said, getting down on one knee. "I know I failed to protect your mother, but—if you'll have me as one of your guards, I swear on my honour that I'll serve you unquestionably and give my life for you."

"You don't have to bow," Daryl said. "And of course I'll have you in my guard, Dad."

Hearing the word *dad* brought a tear to Luthar's eye. How long he had wished to hear those words spoken. "Thank you, Sire . . ."

"Call me Daryl."

"If you insist, Si—Daryl." Luther stood up, smiling.

"'Sorry about your guards," Amanda said, worried. "I didn't . . . kill any, did I?"

"They're all fine," Luthar said, smiling. "A few broken bones, but nothing that won't fix. I think a few of them are more upset that they were knocked out by a woman. Though I must say we'll need to get a new gate made."

"Well," Amanda said, feeling a little smug and flexing one of her arms. "I guess I just didn't know my own strength."

"Indeed," Luthar chuckled. "But we *need* to teach you how to swing a sword properly."

"Amanda," Daryl cried. "Something's happening to Wolvie!"

The moon wolf was surrounded by swirling blue light, which spun round him like a mini tornado. Wolvie turned bright blue and his form seemed to disappear into the light. The wolf seemed to grow as

he stood up on two feet and he transformed into something completely different.

When the light vanished, Wolvie was replaced by a young man with brown hair—and the most beautiful blue eyes that Amanda had ever seen. Her heart stopped, her breath caught—her eyes nearly popped out of her head. The man turned to her, smiling.

"Hello, Amanda."

"Wilfred?" Amanda gasped. "Is . . . is that you?"

"It always was," Wilfred replied.

"Oh," Amanda gasped. "Oh . . ."

Luthar covered Daryl's eyes.

Wilfred walked closer to Amanda. "What Kimera said was true, I did go to him to beg for your safety. He promised me you would remain unharmed—but he betrayed me. After I left you, I met with him in the forest. He stabbed me in the back and left me for dead. I tried to go back to Ashfeld, but I was wounded and didn't get far.

"That's when a druid found me. A kindly, peaceful woman that drew her power from the moon. She offered to use her magic to save me—and she turned me into a moon wolf. I lost all memories of my former life and became her pet, until she passed away from old age.

"I was left alone in the forest, but then I found you and Daryl. I slowly started regaining my memories and . . ." He noticed that Amanda had gone bright red, not knowing where to look. "You're . . . not happy to see me?"

Chapter 16

"Oh no, no, I am . . . ," Amanda stammered. "It's just that . . . er. You, do realise you're naked, don't you?"

Wilfred looked down, gasped and then covered himself as best he could. Luthar hid Daryl behind Amanda and then removed his cloak. "Here." He tied the cloak around Wilfred's waist to hide his shame.

"Thanks," Wilfred stammered, going bright red.

"Between you and me," Luthar whispered, "I can see why Amanda was with you for so long."

Wilfred chuckled, embarrassed. He continued his story. "Where was I? Ah yes. When I found you, I started slowly recovering my memories of you. But it wasn't until I was healed that they returned fully."

"The moon," Luthar said. "I read that the moon heals moon wolves."

Wilfred shook his head. "It wasn't just the moon. Amanda. It was your tear."

Amanda gasped. "My . . . tear . . . ?"

"When I felt your tear against me, all my memories came flooding back. I felt your pain, your—I knew I had to help you get Daryl back. And, I guess now that I've done that, the spell is broken.

"Amanda, what I did was wrong. I left you alone when I should have been there for you. I did it to protect you, but that's no excuse—I turned my back on you when you needed me the most. I promise you, from now on, I'll be there for you every waking second I can be."

Amanda stared at him, her eyes somewhat blank to Wilfred's words. Wilfred wasn't sure how Amanda was reacting to what he was telling her.

"That's, if you'll have me back."

Wilfred wouldn't blame Amanda if she said no. After all, she had suffered and Wilfred had not been there for her. He expected the worse.

Amanda herself was torn. Conflicting emotions ran through her. She was glad to see him again, but also angry. Angry at him, angry at herself. When he left her, her life fell apart—but now that he was back, could she mend it again? Amanda struggled to find the words to try and express how she felt.

But she couldn't find them.

So instead, she threw her arms around Wilfred and kissed him as passionately as she could. "What do you think?" she whispered.

They embraced. Daryl wiped a tear away and even Luthar got a little choked up. Amanda turned back to Daryl. "Well, I guess things *do* have a way of working themselves out," Amanda said.

"Well," Luthar said. "We'd better get your coronation ceremony set up then, My King. It's time Celtland had a proper ruler."

"Well, Daryl," Amanda said. "You're King now, you have it all. You're the ruler of the whole land."

"The *whole* land?" Daryl asked.

"Well, all of Celtland anyway."

"That is so amazing," Daryl gasped. "This is going to be really good, Amanda. You and I are going to have so much fun!"

"Us?"

"Yeah, you and I." He then looked up at Amanda nervously. "You . . . will stay, won't you? You and Wilfred?"

Amanda turned and looked back at Wilfred. Wilfred smiled. She smiled back. Even though they didn't say anything, both knew what the other was thinking. "We'll stay," Amanda replied.

"Yay!" Daryl cried.

"But first . . . I need to do something."

Chapter 17

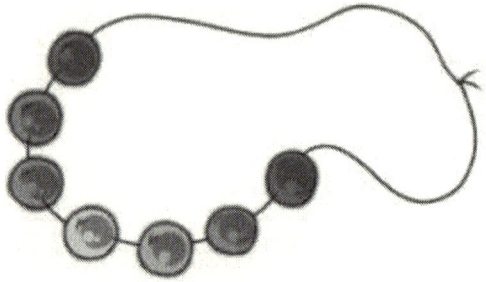

Repaying Old Debts

Ashfeld

Berger swept up the broken debris that Amanda had left in the house, tutting to herself. With all the damage that Amanda had done it would be awhile before it was in a reasonable enough state to sell again. Amanda had really left Berger in a rut—not only did she leave her with ages of back rent, but now she was going to have to pay to get the house fixed up. And she had enough money woes as it was.

She swept the debris across the floor and turned to the doorway, gasping in terror when she saw who was standing there. "Amanda!"

"Hi, Miss Berger," Amanda said meekly.

"You stay back!" Berger cried, holding up the broom.

"I'm not here to cause trouble," Amanda said, holding up her hands.

"You got a lot of nerve coming back here," Berger cried.

"I just want to say something and then I'm gone," Amanda begged. "Please."

"You keep back!" Berger cried. "If you come any closer then I'll thump you one!"

"Is there a problem, Amanda?"

Luthar stepped in after her. He had agreed to come with her to Ashfeld in case there were any problems, whilst Wilfred helped with the coronation ceremony. As soon as Berger saw Luthar, she dropped her broom. "Luthie?"

"Hi, Mum . . . ," Luthar said meekly.

Berger ran up to Luthar, putting her arms around him. "Oh, my baby boy! I've not seen you in ages!"

"Berger is your mum?" Amanda asked, surprised. "Huh, who'd have thought it?"

"What are you doing here, Luthie?"

"I told you not to call me that name," Luthar grunted. "And, I came with Amanda to make sure she was okay."

"You *know* Amanda?"

"Know her? She helped save the King of Celtland. The real King that is."

"She did?"

"Mum, she has something she wants to say, can you please hear her out?"

Berger turned to Amanda, going back to her stern expression and placing her hands on her hips. "All right, it's only because you know my son that I'm hearing you out."

Amanda looked to Luthar. Luthar removed a coin purse from his belt and handed it to Berger. "This is from Amanda," Luthar said.

Berger took the coin purse and looked inside it. "I've . . . I've never seen so many gold coins before."

"It's the back rent I owe you, paid in full," Amanda explained. "Plus for the damages. I'm sorry I took so long to pay you back. I took advantage of your kind nature and I shouldn't have. I just want to make sure that you're paid in full."

"Well, that's very kind of you," Berger said. "And . . . I guess that I have been a little bit unkind to you, given everything that you went through. I should have been a little more understanding. That's on me and I apologise."

"Don't mention it," Amanda said.

Chapter 17

"So, I guess you'll be moving back in soon, I mean as soon as I've cleaned the place up that is?" Berger asked.

Amanda looked around the house, a house that held a lot of memories for her—good and bad. It was still a mess from her rampage before and Berger had only cleaned up a little bit. "You know what," Amanda replied, "someone else can have it."

"You sure?" Berger asked. "Well, if that's what you want. I mean, it will need a huge clean up before I can sell it."

"I can help with that."

Amanda closed her eyes, concentrating her psychokinetic powers on all the damage that she had done. The objects floated around the air, the damaged book case and bottles replaced themselves, the books went back to their places and the scrolls were replaced inside the drawers. In moments, the place looked clean and tidy, as if nothing had ever happened. "There, good as new," Amanda said. "I'll send for my stuff."

"I'll make sure it's ready to go," Berger said. "What about the cot? Will you be taking that too?"

Amanda walked to the spare room, where the cot still remained, covered in cobwebs. Amanda smiled when she remembered that Wilfred spent so much time putting it together, all in preparation for their child. But she would not need it anymore. She blew gently at it, using a gentle blast of air magic to clear the cobwebs from it. It looked as clean and as good as the first day that Wilfred had built it. "Keep it," she told Berger. "It can be part of the house."

Amanda walked past Berger to leave the home, thinking that she had outstayed her welcome. "Amanda," Berger called. "Don't be a stranger. Come back and visit us, okay?"

Coming from Berger, that was actually a pretty good compliment and one that she never expected. "I will," Amanda replied.

Amanda and Luthar emerged from the house. "Luthie?" Amanda asked.

"Please can you not call me that?" Luthar complained. "I hate that name."

"Whatever you say, Luthie," Amanda teased.

Looking ahead, she saw the big man that she owed money to also. He sat by a wall, stroking the stray cat that he found a few days ago. Amanda took a deep breath and sighed. She remembered how last time she nearly killed him and hoped that he wouldn't hold a grudge against her. Luthar stayed behind Amanda in case of trouble.

When the large man saw her coming, he cowered in fear, protecting his cat as well. "No, please don't hurt me!" he cried. "Please, I have a cat with me."

"Hey, hey, it's all right," Amanda said, holding out her hands in peace. "I just want to give you this."

Luthar handed another bag of coins, which she, in turn, held towards the big man.

"What's that?" he asked.

"Your refund," Amanda replied. "Sorry it's late. I put a little extra in there for you, as an apology."

The big man was a little suspicious and seemed to hesitate at first. But he took the bag of gold from her anyway. "Thanks," he said, looking sad. "But it doesn't matter anyway. There isn't much I can do with it."

"Why not?" Amanda asked. "You can buy things for your house."

The big man sighed. "I don't have a house."

"You mean . . . you're homeless?"

"I've tried to get a job so that I can pay for a house, but no one wants me. I hoped that, if I could use the love potion you made to get me a wife, she'd take me in and I'd have a home of my own." He sniffed and his eyes twitched. "I can't even afford to keep Mr. Whiskers fed."

He showed the cat, which was skinny looking and quite weak. It let out a tiny *meow* in pain. Amanda felt so sorry for both of them, and now she understood why he wanted his refund so badly.

A thought came to her. "Captain Luthar," Amanda said. "Don't we need a guard to keep an eye on Kimera?"

Luthar smiled. "I'm sure he'd be perfect."

"Really?" the big man asked, smiling. "You . . . mean that?"

"Yeah, sure, you're a big man and we can use people like you."

"Really?" The big man grabbed Amanda and gave her a big hug with one arm. "Oh, thank you, thank you, thank you!"

"Er, yeah," Amanda stammered, trying not to pass out from his bad breath. "Maybe . . . loosen off a bit, buddy."

"Oh, sorry."

The big man let go of Amanda. "It's okay, really," Amanda replied. "Pleasure to have you, Mr. . . . ."

"Sharon," the big man replied.

"Sharon?" Amanda asked, befuddled.

"My parents always wanted a girl," the big man replied. "But when they found out I was a boy, they couldn't think of any other names."

"Huh," Amanda said.

Chapter 18

The Author

Castle Gryphenpyre

The coronation for Daryl took place later that afternoon. A golden crown was placed on his head whilst Captain Luthar proclaimed him the new King of Celtland. The people cheered, knowing that a time of prosperity was upon them and good times were ahead. Everyone of every major standing was there.

All except one.

"Get me a drink!" Kimera shouted, banging on the prison cell. "I'm thirsty!"

"Hey! Keep it down in there," Sharon shouted back at him. "You're disturbing Mr. Whiskers!"

Sharon fed his cat a piece of chicken. The little creature gobbled it up. Sharon loved his new job at the castle, it meant that he had a warm bed and Mr. Whiskers was fed every night. His life could not be better.

Kimera sat back on the stone slab that was his bed, lined with the roughest of straw. His robes had been stripped from him and he was now wearing an outfit made from potato sacks. He felt so humiliated. He couldn't believe that a person of his standing had to deal with being treated like a common criminal. Him, a King.

Looking around his cell, he gasped as he saw the man in black leaning against the wall, his book open.

"Where did you come from?" Kimera gasped. "Actually, it doesn't matter. You're here now. You can get me out."

"And what opinion did you form that drew you to that conclusion?" the man in black asked.

More bloody riddles! Kimera thought. "Look, you have to get me out of here! Come on, you helped me before, you have to get me out of here."

The man in black looked towards Kimera, his soulless eye making Kimera's blood go cold. "There is a significant difference between helping someone—and letting someone play their part." He closed the book and walked closer to Kimera. "Tell me, what is the difference between a man and a dog?"

"What are you talking about?"

"The difference is that a man leads. A dog follows," the man cut him off. "You picked up the scent of blood like I knew you would and could not help but follow it. But, you should not be surprised—this was always your fate."

Kimera felt his skin crawl and the hairs on the back of his neck stand up. The man's cold, emotionless voice seemed to reach into his heart and squeeze tightly. Kimera suddenly feared for his life, as if the figure before him was a terrible ghul that threatened to swallow his soul.

"Who are you?" he stuttered through chattering teeth.

"Who am I?" the man asked. "As in, you wish to know my name?" the man let out a nasally breath that sounded like a fast snigger. "Names have no meaning to me. A name is simply a false identity that we grant ourselves to give us a sense of belonging. I, on the other hand, have no such illusions. I have been named many things. The Thing That Should Not Be, The Last Firstborn, The Dark Eternal Night—even The Tragic Truth. Who I am is not as much important as *what* I am."

"Then . . . *what* are you?"

"I am the one that prepared this story. I am the one that set you on this path. The one that gives you the illusion of free will, the one that puts words in your mouth and makes you believe that they are your own. I am benevolent to some—malevolent to others.

The Author

"I am, what you might call—an Author."

"I don't understand." Kimera's mind was racing with confusion.

"This whole performance was just a story, and you were my character. A tool to help the narrative to move forward. But now your role is almost at an end."

Kimera had no clue as to what this "Author" was talking about. But he saw that The Author was not paying him any attention and was more interested in his book. "What is that you're reading? Why do you carry it around with you?"

The Author closed the book and held it closer to the light. The book was pure black and smooth, but Kimera thought that he could see a slight circular indent in the middle of it, like something small and round should have been held in it, but it was missing. There were other indents above it, but they seemed too faint for Kimera to see what they were.

"This tome," The Author started, "contains everything that was, everything that is and everything that will be."

Kimera's frustration at being able to understand The Author got the better of him and his fear subsided temporarily. He jumped to his feet and pointed a finger at him. "I've had enough of your riddles and nonsense! You had better tell me what is going on. And I demand to see what that book is."

"You may," The Author said. "But I doubt that you will enjoy what you see."

He threw the book at Kimera, hitting his belly. The thing felt like it weighed a ton; Kimera didn't see how The Author was able to hold it so easily. Kimera laid it on his lap and opened the pages. The paper felt rough and old, as if they would tear with the slightest pull.

Kimera riffled through the pages of the enormous tome. The writing was in some strange language that he didn't understand, and the more he looked at it, the more it hurt his head. There were also pictures to go along with the text so he spent more time looking at them.

One picture showed Kimera with his sister Sheena as she was crowned Queen—and the jealous look in his eyes. The next showed Sheena and Luthar together as Daryl—as a baby—was carried to safety. Another showed him at the village. Him meeting with The Author. And his final battle with Amanda. The last page he dared to look at was him in the cell with The Author.

Chapter 18

Kimera would not have thought twice about this, after all The Author could have easily put these in here.

Except that the ink on the page had been dry for centuries—and the paper was equally as old.

"How . . . ," Kimera gasped. "How is this possible?"

"Some stories are so powerful that they have to be told," The Author replied. "You were just another part of Amanda's catharsis."

Even though The Author showed no emotion when he spoke, Kimera picked up on the slightest of feeling when The Author said "Amanda." Admiration maybe? Or love?

"Amanda," Kimera snarled. Even just *thinking* of the name of the woman that ruined everything made his blood boil. "Why is she so important? I must know!"

He riffled ahead of the book, storming through the pictures as if his life depended on it. He needed to know more about Amanda and why The Author seemed to care so much.

And as he got to the last page, he saw what Amanda's fate would be.

His hair turned white, his pupils dilated and he breathed a fearful breath.

The Author picked up the book from Kimera's catatonic body, looking at the page that Kimera had been looking at.

"That's the problem with reading ahead," The Author smirked, closing the book with a bang. "Sometimes you discover knowledge that you wish you hadn't."

The Forest of Celt, Six Years Ago

Sheena couldn't believe that she was still alive. Looking up towards the top of the cliff, she estimated that she must have fallen at least two hundred feet or so. By all accounts, pieces of her should have been spread out across the land now. But, as she fell, it was like a powerful gust of air had cushioned her, gradually ending her descent until she landed gently. She didn't understand how—or why. The dragons must have been watching over her.

The ground that she lay on was soggy and her dress was caked with mud. A stream was ahead of her, the river roaring fiercely down it. Daryl remained in her arms, which she counted her blessings a thousand times over. He was crying, but still alive. Sheena held him close to her, whispering calming words into his ears. She tried to

162

stand, but the burning pain from the wound Kimera had given her, mixed with the soggy mud below, meant that she couldn't get a clear footing and fell down. Her dress had turned a crimson colour and she lost more blood with each passing second.

Kimera, she thought, remembering the treachery of her brother. She didn't know how he had rallied her own soldiers against her—but she was going to be certain to make him pay for this. And this time, she was not going to be so lenient.

She tried to stand up again, but the soggy mud once again hindered her progress. She kept one arm on Daryl, making sure that he was never out of her grip for a single second. She looked ahead of her, almost certain that she could see the outline of a figure. At first, she thought it was just shadows—but when the thunder struck and lit up the area, she definitely could see someone standing there.

"Hello?" Sheena called out. "Hello? Help me, please."

The man walked closer to Sheena and she saw that his clothing was just as dark as the night sky. The only light on his outfit was the half mask that he wore, that was just nearly hidden under his dark hat. His one eye looked towards Sheena with neither malice nor pity. In fact, there was no emotion in his look at all. He looked bone dry, despite the cold rain lashing down—almost as if the elements themselves were afraid to touch him. Sheena's fear heightened—but Daryl's cry brought her round and she remembered her predicament. She had to take a chance to see if this man was friend or foe.

"Please," Sheena said. "I'm hurt. I . . . I need to get back to Celtland. I'm . . . you have to help me, please . . . my baby . . ."

The Author knelt down beside Sheena, his single eye never leaving her. Sheena could feel her heart beating a million times a second. She could not sense anything from this man, so she didn't know if he meant any ill will to her or not. The Author reached one hand towards her—but when Sheena thought he was going to take hold of her, his hands wrapped around Daryl. With a superhuman tug, The Author ripped Daryl from Sheena's grip. Sheena felt her blood go cold, feeling nothing but air where her baby was.

"No," she cried as The Author stood up and backed away. "My baby! Give me back my baby!"

Sheena frantically tried to get to her feet, but the soggy earth stopped her. She clawed at The Author's trousers, like a lion trying to rip apart an enemy. She beat against him, hoping to gain enough strength to break his legs and send him down so that she would be with her son again.

"Give me back my child!"

The Author was impervious to her screams, but Daryl, panicked by the loud noises, started crying. Sheena started crying also, feeling her child's pain.

"Please . . . give him back to me."

The Author raised one eye to a man standing behind her.

"Kill her."

Sheena felt something cold and sharp against her throat.

It danced across her neck.

Her body fell into the river, carried on downstream.

Marcus dropped the knife from his hands, barely able to keep back his tears. He turned to The Author, who looked back at him with the blankest of all stares. He handed the child to his disciple, though Marcus struggled to keep a grip on the baby—his hands shook too much.

"You will raise this child as your own," The Author ordered him. "When the time is right, he will leave you. Until then, say nothing of this."

"Yes . . . Master," Marcus stammered. "Master . . . my wife . . . will she—"

"When you return, you will find your wife in perfect health, as promised," The Author replied.

The Author turned around and walked away, the wind and rain not touching any part of him. Now all he had to do was wait until the next chapter began. Everything was proceeding as he had wanted it to.

Chapter 19

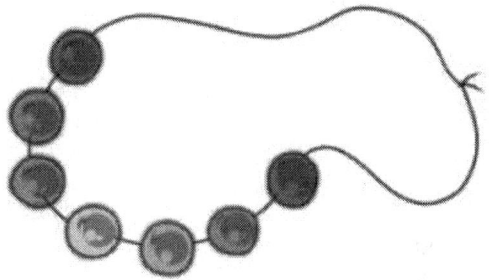

Happiness at Last

Castle Gryphenpyre

Amanda pulled the bed sheets across Daryl, making sure he was tucked in. It was a huge double bed that he slept in now with golden and silver covers. It was somewhat larger than was necessary for a boy of his size, but it would offer him comfort.

"I've never seen a bed this big before," Daryl exclaimed. "This can't be all for me."

"It is," Amanda replied. "Perks of being King you see."

Daryl let out a heavy yawn; it had been a very long day and he was tired. "What do we do tomorrow then?"

"Whatever you want," Amanda replied. "You're King now, you can do whatever you please. I spoke to Luthar. he told me that me and Wilfred can stay here at the castle as your Regents."

"Regents?"

"Legally you need a Regent to act in your stead until you come of age," Amanda replied. "I asked Luthar if he would like to be a Regent, but he told me he would be too busy with his duty as a Captain. So he gave the position to me and Wilfred. I guess you could say we'll be your guardians."

"My guardians? Does . . . does that mean I can call you Mum?"

Mum. A word that Amanda never thought she would ever be called. Hearing it made her heart go all aflutter. She stroked his forehead. "You can call me anything you want."

Amanda kissed Daryl on the forehead. Her lips had barely left his skin when she felt Daryl's arms wrap around her shoulders. "What's that for?" Amanda asked, somewhat caught off guard.

"I just wanted to hug you," Daryl replied.

Smiling, Amanda put her arms around Daryl's shoulders to repay the favour. "I'm so glad that you stayed," Daryl whispered in her ear.

"Me too," Amanda replied.

Daryl yawned again and Amanda figured it was time to let Daryl sleep. She let him down onto the pillow and then pulled the sheet over him again. "Goodnight, Daryl."

She put out the candle near his bed and then got up to leave. "I love you Amanda," Daryl said as she opened the door to leave.

Amanda stopped, caught off guard somewhat. She turned back and smiled. "I love you too, Daryl."

She closed the door behind her gently, leaving Daryl to rest. Luthar and a few guards were stationed outside. "He's asleep."

"I'll keep watch over him," Luthar replied. "Thank you for saving my son. If there is anything I can do to repay you . . ."

"Actually, there is."

"Name it."

Amanda took her necklace of dragon gems, removing the Blood gem and handed it to Luthar. "Put this away somewhere safe. Somewhere no one can get to it."

"Are you sure?" Luthar asked. "This could be a pretty useful gem to have, if you learn to control it."

Amanda shook her head. "It's too much of a burden. No one should have to bear it."

Luthar nodded. "I'll see to it that it's put away safely."

"I can take it, sir," a nearby guard said.

"Thank you," Luthar said, handing it over to the guard. "Make sure no one can get to it. And be careful with it."

"Aye, sir."

The guard left, taking the gem. He passed by Wilfred, who was making his way to Amanda. "Is he asleep now?" Wilfred asked.

Amanda nodded.

"Amanda, do you still have that ring?"

She dug into a pocket in her dress, pulling out the diamond ring that Wilfred had given her. It still sparkled as if it contained a magic from within.

"That's good," Wilfred said. "We'll need it for the wedding."

"Wedding? Whose wedding?"

Wilfred smiled. Amanda gasped.

"Wait a minute," she said suddenly. "After what you did, what makes you think I'd say yes?"

"Well, I did consider that," Wilfred said. "But then, I already had ordered a really nice blue suit and a golden wedding dress for yourself. And I invited all our friends and got a really nice feast planned. But . . . if you're not interested I could always cancel."

"Don't you dare," Amanda said, scowling.

"I thought that would be your answer."

Amanda could barely contain herself. "I can't believe that I'm hearing this."

"Well, it seems appropriate," Wilfred said. "After all . . . you gave me the most magical time."

Amanda reached up and ran her fingers through Wilfred's soft brown hair. "And you gave me a wonderful time."

She pulled Wilfred close and pressed her lips against his.

Amanda and Wilfred pulled away from the kiss and they looked at each other. He looked so handsome in his blue suit, made from the finest materials in all the land. He almost seemed to sparkle like a diamond. Amanda herself was beautiful in her golden wedding dress. She had never looked more radiant.

"I hereby pronounce you both married," the priest exclaimed.

A thunderous applause came from the people inside the hall, filled to the brim with the guests they had invited. Everyone that they could fit into the hall, be they Lord or peasant, was here to witness this momentous occasion. Luthar was at the front, clapping and smiling, Sharon and Mr. Whiskers were cheering also—even Berger

Chapter 19

had come from Ashfeld to see them. She blew into a handkerchief as her tears fell.

Daryl, the King of Celtland, walked up to them. He was dressed in green robes with a long cape, the crown resting snugly on his head—like it was made for him. He was so proud of them. His two favourite people, together at last.

Wilfred picked the King up and rested him between him and Amanda. Everyone was on their feet, roaring with applause. The cheers that followed were powerful and showed the appreciation of everyone here today. All for Wilfred and Amanda.

Amanda felt tears fall from her eyes.

But, for the first time in ages, they were tears of happiness.

Happiness at Last

Epilogue

The End?

Castle Gryphenpyre

The guard turned down an empty corridor, chucking the Blood gem up and down in his hand and catching it, treating it as nothing more than a normal stone despite the warning from his Captain.

He threw it up in the air at least three times.

The third time that it dropped, black gloves caught it.

The lifeless body of the guard disappeared like sand in the wind. The Author held the Blood gem close to his one good eye. He was in awe of the raw power this gem possessed, which even dwarfed his own. And yet, he knew its full power had not been unleashed.

He looked at the last page of his black book. The picture showed Amanda standing with a wall of fire behind her. Her eyes appeared like two exploding suns. At her feet were corpses—one with a hole where the heart should have been, another with his head twisted so far that his neck was broken, the other burned beyond all recognition. There were other bodies in the picture, but these ones stood out the most.

In the picture, around her neck, was a single gem.

The Author closed the book and placed the Blood gem in the small gap on the front cover. The gem fit perfectly and lit up. The small indents above it were lit and were filled with a bright orange colour, which appeared to burn like molten lava. The filled up indents made up words—or rather a title.

Moonstone Falls.

Thanks for reading!

We hoped you enjoyed this novel.

What follows is a short teaser for the
second novel in the series:

Amanda
Moonstone
THE DARKBANE
SORCERESS

Coming 2016

Sample Chapter

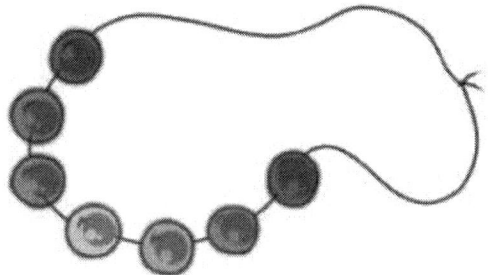

The Darkbane Sorceress

O *f all the magic that existed in our world—and may say still exist to this very day—none is more terrifying and dangerous than that of dark magic. The legends state that it was the tool of Abadon herself, a seductive weapon promising power and glory to any who used it. But, to use such power came with a price. For to activate this power, one had to access the darkness within their very soul. All the wickedness and cruelty of that person was increased ten-fold and their sanity was shattered. Those who wielded dark sorcery desired nothing but power over everything else. They were feared across the whole planet—just to mention the name of a dark magic user was enough to turn even the bravest men white as snow.*

And none were more terrifying than that of Lady Saevitia Darkbane—The Darkbane Sorceress.

Born to the land of Celtland, it was said that her parents were leaders of a monstrous cult. Followers of Abadon, Darkbane knew only darkness from the time she was born. So much so that, when she was only five years old, she murdered her own parents and became the most powerful of dark sorceress's users. Her cruelty was every bit as legendary as that of her parents and she would attack villages, raid homes, steal children from their beds–all so that she could use them as sacrifices for her vile spells.

Something had to be done. And it fell to King Harod of the Gryphenpyre household to destroy her once and for all. But her influence had grown. Any attempt on her was met with failure. The King grew desperate and turned to the Republic of Garmany for help. Fortune favoured them as the cities of Drewghaven and Valenco gifted them a weapon that was a result of both industry and alchemy. It was called "The Cleanser".

This weapon fired a shell that was charged with powerful magic, launching it towards Saevitia. But even this was not enough to destroy Lady Darkbane. Her vengeance was devastating and many fell to her grip. It came down to an unknown warrior–know only as the Great Shadori Warrior–who fought and destroyed Lady Darkbane once and for all. But the warrior disappeared and his name has now been lost to time...

Sample taken from the novel *The Magic of Draconica: A tale of Sorcery.*

Shadowraven Castle, Eighteen Years Later

Foliage parted as the dark soldiers carefully made their way through the forest, their long white hair gently breezing in the wind whilst their green eyes gazed ahead. Their skin was purple and they were clad head to toe in black clothing, with some outlines of red. Some wore hoods, some wore light armour whilst others had hoods over their heads and some kept their mouths covered with black cloths. Many of them had scabbards on their backs which held slightly curbed blades, but some had two. They moved in complete silence like living shadows–their presence was such that even the night animals were afraid to make a sound.

They moved out into a clearing into the forest and a black hand at the front halted the movement of the shadow. Their leader wore a long black coat that stopped just above his feet, held in place with two spiked shoulder pads. Underneath the coat was armour that followed the same red and black colour scheme as the rest of his warriors. Unlike the others, his outfit covered virtually all his flesh, the only part of his body visible was white hair that was tied back and hung out the back of his helmet. And what a sight his helmet was to behold—it was like a monster that had stepped out of the Necroworld, red spikes adorned the head and two rubies in the eye sockets burned like fire when light of the full moon hit them. On his back were two curved swords, much like those of the others—except the blades were dark crimson, like they had just been dipped in hot blood.

The leader lowered his hand and appeared to look ahead, sniffing the air. There was a large castle directly in front of him, several feet away. It was built from rock as black as night and was barely illuminated by the moonlight. But from what was shown it was clear that this castle was in a state of decay, abandoned for many centuries. Its rocks were jagged and crumbling, many had already worn away from centuries of wear and weather. It was less like a castle and more like a ruin—left alone for as long as anyone could remember. And with good reason. This castle was considered an ill omen by many in Celtland and they stayed away from it wherever possible.

Underneath his mask, the leader grinned. He knew there was no doubt that this was where they had to go. He moved his hand forward, signaling to his brothers to move on. The shadow bound ahead, creeping towards the castle like moths to a flame.

The warriors met with no resistance when they entered the crumbling relic and they walked down the hallway. The leader could smell damp in his nose and water dripped from the castle walls. The inside of the castle was just as shocking as the outside. Many walls had gaping holes where stone had fallen off or rotted away. Cobwebs lined the nooks and crannys of the walls; the spiders having made their homes here now. The place was in a terrible state and it would take more than just a touch up to fix its problems. In fact, it would have been better to let the whole thing crumble and build the whole thing up from scratch. Torches were lined up against the wall, light brightly to guide the warriors along. Although the leader knew that the torches had only been lit recently. They smelled brand new compared to the rest of the castle. Their contact had to be here.

They followed the light of the torches until they reached a giant chamber. Broken black pillars littered the ground and moonlight poured in from the giant hole in the roof. At the end of the chamber was a large, throne; the gold rusted from many years of neglect. It currently had an occupant sitting on it, relaxing on the chair as comfortably as any Queen could. The light from the roof avoided this person and all they could see in the darkness was her glowing, purple eyes. She looked up as the shadows stopped with their leader, speaking to them in a deep tone that was feminine—but threatening.

"*You're late.*"

The leader was somewhat surprised that she spoke in his native tongue, it was almost enough to distract him from the crassness of her remark. "*You speak Shadorian?*" His voice was husky and somewhat muffled by the mask he wore.

"*A have spent time in your country,*" the figure replied. "*That is how I came to find out about the Singing Screams and their leader, Vladric the Butcher.*"

"Butcher *General*," the leader of the clan corrected, this time speaking in Commonspeak.

"My mistake," the dark figure on the throne responded.

"I must say that you have picked an... interesting spot to meet," Vladrac replied, looking around. Though he could not see the castle, being that he no longer had eyes to see, his other senses were painting him a picture clearer than sight could ever paint.

"This castle used to belong to Lord Shadowraven," the figure replied. "During the Age of Sorcery, he was one of the most powerful mages to ever have mastered dark magic. For over two hundred years he remained unchallenged. This is all that remains of his legacy. But that is not the reason I chose this spot."

"I must say that when I got the message via raven, I was taken by surprise. It is rare that we ever get hired for our services outside our own country," Vladrac said. "So tell me, who would summon us here?"

The figure stood up from the throne and walked towards the light, her feet echoing across the old rock. The bottom half of her purple dress was the first that came into view, the light moving up her body as she moved closer. It moved up her waist and then to her chest, revealing a lock of black hair draped over her shoulders, a golden headband on her forehead. A dark purple cloak dragged behind her, attached to a spindly ruff around her neck and a collar that stood rigidly behind her head. Her skin was somewhat paler than most flesh tones and her cheekbones made the bottom half of her face a little flat. The pupils of her purple eyes were like a single line of black, like cats eyes.

"My name is Saevitia Darkbane," the figure replied. "One hundred years ago, I was betrayed and my people murdered by the Gryphenpyre household. Now I have been granted a second life and I intend to use it for one purpose–revenge."

"I have heard of you, sorceress," Vladrac murmured, hardly sounding phased by what had been told to him. "But how can I be sure that you are who you say you are?"

The left side of Saevitia's lips curled slightly. She lifted up both hands and they came alight with dark energy, burning in the night like a start. The Singing Screams gasped and stepped back. This was dark magic in its purest form. A raging maelstrom of power and devastation in the palm of her hands.

"Impressive," Vladrac said, feeling the heat of the dark energy. "I have no cause now to distrust you."

The other side of Saevitia's lips curled, making a smile.

"But tell me, My Lady. Why did you contact us? If the legends are true, your powers are quite formidable."

Saevitia dispelled the magic from her hand. "There was a time when that was true, yes. There was a time when a click of my fingers could create an earthquake that would destroy a city. A time when I could rip the very sky asunder and make fire rain from the heavens. There was even a time when I could just incinerate entire legions with a point of my finger." Her rodomontade disappeared as suddenly as it appeared. "But... My powers have diminished and they are still not at full strength. It will be days before I have regained everything. Maybe even weeks. Or years... But my thirst for vengeance will not wait that long. It MUST be sated! That is why I need you."

"You have been wise in your choice," Vladrac said, placing a hand to his chest and bowing lightly. "But, I fear that I must bring attention we *are* mercenaries. And as such our services are not paid with faith alone."

Saevitia had expected no less. She had heard that the Singing Screams were known for their unquenchable greed as much as their thirst for blood. It was always a danger when hiring the Singing Screams as, whilst they would get the job done, there was a terrible consequence should you ever cheat them out of payment. Fortunately, Saevitia had come prepared. She unattached a bag from her belt and threw it to Vladrac, who caught it.

"Your down payment," Saevitia said.

Vladrac clicked his fingers and the nearest Singing Scream assassin came forward. He handed him the bag and he opened it to look inside. Diamonds sparkled from within. He took one out and looked at it until he was satisfied. "It's real diamond, Butcher General."

Vladrac smiled underneath his helmet. "What is your command, San-Sai?"

Saevitia smiled. "We will attack the city of Wrightson at dawn. We will hit the city and take the King."

"You want us to take a whole city?" Vladrac asked, almost like a sneer. "And here I thought you were going to ask us to do something difficult."

"You sound confident," Saevitia said. "I should warn you that, from what I heard, the military is trained by a war hero. They are the best soldiers in the entire country."

"No training can prepare them for my warriors," Vladrac sneered.

"Good, then we shall attack Wrightson at first light and catch them unaware. I also need you to find something for me. Something of-"

"Mummy!"

Saevitia turned round. A small child no older than six, with dark hair and wearing a purple romper suit was behind her, glaring angrily. Saevitia put a hand to the side of her head, sighing. "What is it, Sammy?"

"You said you'd read me a bedtime story!" the boy pouted.

"Look, Mummy is very busy at the moment," Saevitia tried to explain.

"But you *promised*!" Sammy shouted, stamping his foot.

"Look, just give me ten minutes, okay?" Saevitia begged. "Then I'll read you a story, I promise."

"That's what you said two hours ago," Sammy whined, his eyes becoming wet with tears. "You never make ANY time for me!"

He charged off, wailing at the top of his lungs. "I hate you! I hate you! I hate you! I HATE you!"

Saevitia tried to call out for Sammy, but he had already disappeared from her sight.

Great, now I got to go back to THAT, she thought.

Sometimes it wasn't easy planning her revenge *and* being a single mother.

Remembering her guests, she turned back to them, trying not to look sheepish. "Sorry about that. Um, where was I? Yes, I remember. Vladrac, are you prepared to do what I order?"

"Without question, San-Sai," Vladrac replied.

"Excellent," Saevitia sneered. "The Gryphenpyre family will pay dearly for the pain they have caused me. They will soon know what it feels like to burn."

END OF SAMPLE

Acknowledgements and Notes

There are a ton of people that I want to thank for helping and inspiring me. But first I wanted to let you guys know a little about the book you've just read for the sake of those that may be new to my writings.

Amanda Moonstone was written as a companion piece to my main series, *Draconica*. Some of you that are familiar with my work may have noticed some little nods and mentions of characters from that series (if you didn't, not to worry—the glossary will clue you in). In case you are wondering, yes the events of *Amanda Moonstone* take place in the same period as the *Draconica* series. Whereabouts I hear you ask? Well if you look at the clues within the novel, it should be pretty easy to spot.

But anyway I've got a lot of people to thank for this book so let's not waste any time.

First and foremost, I want to thank the authors at Paper Crane Books for their support. So thank you Holly Bardo, Michelle Franklin and Morgan Straughan Comnick—who has also helped me with my Youtube series *Totalitarian Warlords and Termination Squadron*. Morgan, I really hope one day someone from a major film or animation studio snaps you up as you are as talented a voice actor as you are a writer. ☺

And of course, thanks to the wonderful Sheenah Freitas. Your proofreading and edits were fantastic and I hope I wasn't too much of a pain in the butt!

I would also like to thanks to my family for their support. To my parents Mary and Malcolm, thank you both for help with the story. I also wanna thank my brother Ben for being so cool and of course, my cat Whispa—even if she did jump on my keyboard causing me to lose an entire chapter one time!

I would also would like to thank my "Disciples" Charmaine Pitchford, Tom Woodman, Victoria Collins, Franz Alli, Reilina Villacarlos, Will Turner, Brian Wilkerson and anyone else who has plugged me on Facebook, become a patron to my work or sponsored my writing. You guys rock and I really cannot thank you enough! If I missed anyone out I apologise.

A special shout out to Kirsten Moody—aka Snow The Wanderer—my wonderful artist for this project! The artwork and her dedication to this project has been nothing short of amazing. Thank you for being a part of this!

And last, but by no means least, thank you so much for reading this novel and continuing to support indie authors out there. I hope you guys enjoyed reading *Amanda Moonstone: The Missing Prince* as much as I did writing it and Sheenah did editing it! XD.

Much love,
Dan Wright

Glossary of Terms

The following is a brief explanation of the various terms mentioned in *Amanda Moonstone: The Missing Prince*.

Adamtine Mines: A recently discovered set of mines nearby Cantasham. Named after the Adamtine family, who discovered them in the year 15 NE

Age of Science: The time proceeding The Age of Sorcery. Occurred in the year c.4500 OE (although this date is fiercely debated amongst many Draconican scholars). Refers to the time when Dronor (see below) taught the humans to use the natural resources of the planet and forget the old ways of magic. With this, they learned to use the natural resources of the planet (which helped them build cities, create medicine and forge weapons amongst other things) rather than relying on magic, which was unpredictable and often dangerous.

Age of Sorcery: The time preceding The Age of Science. In this time, humans used magic for everyday life. But due to the dangers of magic, it caused a lot of problems and few could control it effectively. After magic caused unnecessary destruction to the planet, the dragon Dronor taught the people of the world how to use the natural resources as an alternative source. This began The Age of Science.

Alchemy: A study of both magic and science. Whilst magic is generally looked down upon, alchemy looks at the concept of using magic within the realms of scientific possibility, thus making it acceptable in most cultures. Alchemy also teaches how to mix potions for various different means—which ranges from medicinal to weaponized potions.

Ashfeld: The home of Amanda Moonstone. Used to be a fairly quiet town before The Incident (see below).

Baalaria: Also known as The Baalarian Empire. The country of Baalaria is set in the northern lands, but the empire as a whole refers to Baalaria, Ira-Kai and parts of Shadoria. One of the most powerful military forces on the planet, it was responsible for The Gothon Campaign in 10 NE (see below).

Blood gem: Supposedly the only one of its kind left. Blood magic was said to be one of the most dangerous of all the magics. After the Age of Sorcery, all links to Blood magic was supposedly destroyed. How Amanda came into contact with this gem is as yet unknown— but she has kept hold of it knowing how much damage it could do in the wrong hands.

Brittana: Celtland's neighbouring country. A country built on chivalry and strong moral principles. Its current ruler is Queen Daniar Dragonkin.

Cantasham: A large town in Celtland, governed by Lord Adamtine. Very popular for tradespeople and extremely wealthy thanks to the discovery of the Adamtine mine.

Celtland: The country in which *Amanda Moonstone* takes place. Neighbouring country to Brittana, it is a country that is rich in beautiful forests and the people are known for their love of nature.

Cromiweed: A dark green plant. Its seeds are said to trigger a hallucinatory effect on the user. Was supposedly fed to berserkers before they went into battle.

Daniar Dragonkin: The Queen of Brittana and one of the Dragonkin. A legendary warrior that fought during The Gothon Campaign. Was also a close friend to Sheena Gryhenpyre. Her dragon power is fire.

Draconica: The planet in which *Amanda Moonstone* takes place on. Said to have been founded by the dragons (see below) and has existed for over five thousand years—though this is sometimes hotly debated amongst scholars.

Dragon: A race of powerful creatures that could travel through Time and Space itself. They created life on Draconica based on the other worlds they visited—or so the legends go. Now extinct.

Dragon gems: Gems that contain various magical powers. Can grant the users certain powers if they have the skill to use magic.

Dragonkin: A human/dragon hybrid created by Dronor to carry on the name of the dragons. They have different powers depending on which dragon they represent.

Dronor: The last of the dragons who created the Dragonkin. His death is the starting point of the New Era (see below).

Dunaway River: The largest river that runs through the Forest of Celt. Said to have magical properties. Dunaway village was set up next to it.

Forest of Celt: The largest forest on Draconica. Separates Brittana and Celtland. Generally considered a peaceful place, though there are some dangerous areas.

Ghul: A creature created from magic. Comes in all shapes and sizes, often appearing in elemental form. They are mindless and will attack anything on sight. Weaker ghuls can be destroyed fairly easily, but stronger ghuls can only be destroyed by magic.

The Gothon Campaign: Refers to a time then the Baalarian Empire began worldwide conquest, under the command of the tyrannical Emperor Erik Gothon III (to which The Gothon Campaign was named after). Lasted between 9–10 NE. Celtland was one of the countries invaded during this war and, as a result, they don't trust the Baalarian Empire, despite the recent peace from the country.

Gryhenpyre: One of the oldest royal families in Celtland. Their name is derived from the sigil of a bear with wings which was a mythical creature that was also called a gryhenpyre. A family that is (for the most part) held in high regard amongst the Celtland people and their bloodline has ruled for over 200 years. In legend, gryhenpyres had golden fur, but on occasion they gave birth to black coloured gryhenpyres. There are some that believe that the gryhenpyre, as an animal, would sometimes mate with normal bears, as opposed to their own species. Black gryhenpyres were therefore considered "illegitimate" and not fully part of their family.

The Ice Maiden: A famous children's book on Draconica, written by Kristoff Hanna Elsasven (a renowned author from Drewghaven). It tells a story of a woman that freezes everything that crosses her path, but in the end true love brings her round. Said to be loosely based on Zarracka Dragonkin, whom Elsasven was said to be romantically involved with. Some believe that this was meant to portray Zarracka in a more positive light, given her notoriety—but none have managed to prove this as yet.

The Incident: Refers to a time in Ashfeld c.16 NE where Amanda Moonstone, under the influence of the Blood gem, went berserk and destroyed much of the town. No one was reported to be hurt and Amanda was eventually calmed down by her then lover Wilfred. Much to the annoyance of the townsfolk, Amanda seemed to be given a pardon for her actions (though the truth behind this was much more sinister) and since then Amanda became somewhat of a social outcast.

Kerrigal: The dragon that discovered magic and introduced it to the planet. Killed during a fight with Dronor.

Magic: A mystical force that was discovered by the dragons deep in the core of Draconica. Kerrigal taught the humans to use it in everyday life—thus beginning The Age of Sorcery. However, in its rawest form, magic is unpredictable and extremely difficult to control. As a result, Draconica suffered a lot of damage over a period of time. Dronor decided to teach the mortals to use the resources of the planet and as such, The Age of Science was created. Nowadays, magic is looked down upon by many societies—although variations like alchemy are accepted. For those that still follow magic, there are various items that allow them to manipulate it—although only a certain number can actually use these items. There is some that believe that one has to be "Born into Magic" to be able to use magic items. Magic in its purest form cannot be controlled without causing great harm to humans and, to date, there has only been a handful of people able to use pure magic. However, much of what Draconicans know of magic is mostly speculation as few reliable texts about magic exist. The people of Draconica may never know the true purpose or meaning behind magic—nor do some of them want to.

Monkeybadger: A light Draconican insult. Usually used to describe someone who is annoying and/or stupid.

Moon wolf: Supposedly extinct wolves that were said to be the children of the moon. Moonlight could heal them. Stories go that they were created by moon druids, who would turn injured mortals to wolves to serve as their guardians or pets. However, the story goes that moon wolves could turn back to humans if they redeemed themselves for a past mistake in their lives.

Moonstone Falls: ???

New Era: Abbreviation NE. Refers to the date when Dronor, the last of the dragons, died and Draconica had to now live in a world where dragons didn't exist. All dates in the NE are listed chronologically.

Old Era: Abbreviation OE. Refers to the time prior to Dronor's death, when the dragons still lived. All dates here are listed in reverse. The oldest recorded date on Draconican record is c.5000 OE. However, some historians claim that Draconica as a planet has been around much longer than that and that there was life *before* the dragons. This is a subject that is open to debate.

Roseflower: A red-coloured flower that is mainly used in medicines. Usually used for a sedative due to the calming feel it gives users.

Royal Blessing: When the reigning (or acting) monarch grants a soldier access into the Royal Guard. Said to be the greatest honour any soldier can be given.

Royal Guard: The personal soldiers/bodyguard to the Crown.

Valenco: A county from the Republic of Garmany. The world leader in alchemy, its University is highly renowned for producing top alchemists.

Watergate Pass: A small village set outside the Forest of Celt. Some say that it is named Watergate Pass as no river runs nearby it, leading the villagers to venture out to get water.

Wrightson: The capital city of Celtland. Named after the first King of Celtland—Malcolm Wrightson.

Zarracka Dragonkin: Possibly the most infamous of all the Dragonkin. Zarracka once tried to burn down the capital of Brittana and also allied with the Baalarian Empire during The Gothon Campaign. Said to be one of the most alluring of all women, she is nevertheless held in ill repute, though it is said that she was romantically involved with author Kristoff Hanna Elsasven. She is currently serving an indefinite jail sentence under the command of Queen Daniar. Her dragon powers were ice.

A note about titles: in Draconican lore, titles such as King, Queen, Lord, Prince, etc. always have the first letter capitalised, regardless of which context they are used. This is to show their importance and higher ranking than common folk.

About the Author
(the ACTUAL author, not the character!)

Dan lives Canterbury, Kent, UK. He picked up a love of Fantasy stories after reading *The Lord of the Rings*, *The Lion, The Witch and the Wardrobe* and numerous Roald Dahl novels. He is best known for his Draconica series, a Fantasy/Manga series that has been praised for its Anime style action, humour and illustrations. He has also had a short comic strip called *Queller*, which was published in an anthology for the comic *Lighting Strike Presents* . . . and has also been a judge for a book competition at his local school.

Dan also runs various websites dedicated to the world of Draconica, a blog and he occasionally reviews books. His other hobby is playing guitar in a band called Rage of Silence. He likes all kinds of music—but he mainly listens to rock and metal, rap, some pop music and also film and video game scores. He also loves Disney and Pixar movies—often finding himself singing along to the tunes, or crying manly tears!

He is also a slave to his cat, who takes up a lot of his time when he isn't at work or writing!

To learn more about Dan, visit him at the following places:

Blog: http://pandragondan.weebly.com
Draconica Website: http://draconicaseries.weebly.com
Amanda Website: http://moonstonefalls.weebly.com
Facebook: https://www.facebook.com/PandragonDanWright
                 https://www.facebook.com/AmandaMoonstoneSeries
                 https://www.facebook.com/TrappedonDraconica
Twitter: @PandaDanWright

Made in the USA
Charleston, SC
24 July 2015